Executive Dishwasher 360 Degrees of Culinary

A Cookbook Novel

by

Brittany Wallace

&

Jonathan Penright

2022

<u>**Table of Contents**</u>

ACKNOWLEDGMENTS

To my family both earthly and spiritual you already know the love is strong, may the legacy be carved with a chef knife. To all of the Master Teachers, thank you for sharing your wisdom, I am forever a student. A special thank you to The Culinary Institute of Lenotre for providing great value and then some. The experience was pivotal to my growth as a chef and the 2 years I dedicated there will forever shape my walk. A very special thank you for the forgiveness I've received over the years, my mistakes have been many. To all of my fans and loved ones that have been rooting for me, I hope this places a big smile on your face. Enjoy!

-   *Jonathan J Penright*

To my parents and family, for raising me with love and ambition and for encouraging me to always set and achieve new goals. To my circle of friends and supporters, for inspiring me to dream bigger, for being my safe place and never letting me forget exactly how loved I am.

Writing this book has challenged me in so many ways, and I'm incredibly humbled and grateful to have been a part of it. My hope is that this story inspires readers to try something new, and challenges them to know themselves better.

-   *Brittany Wallace*

Chapter 1

Horizon

Before the time of online applications, when you had to walk into a restaurant to apply for a job, there was always one position sitting on the corner like the bottom street walker just before the 1st of the month. In a lot of cases you could get started that very same day, as long as your criminal record isn't too violent of course. Petty drug offenses… pst… Everybody in the kitchen is on something or should be, or isn't on anything and is a psychopath serial killer that oddly gets overly excited when carving a lamb. The culinary industry at times can be a bottom scraper, filtering through the outcast and misfits that can't quite get it together enough "from an economic societal perspective" to not have to scrub pots and pans while everybody else is eating or enjoying some social event with their loved ones. I thought I would avoid the dishwasher experience by going to culinary school and coming in as an officer in the industry, yet my very first Executive Chef position at Bay Oaks Country Club had me washing mountains of dishes, it was pathetic. It makes you put some respect on the title Dishwasher.
– Kababo

Every once in a while, not so often that people came to expect it, but often enough that they had something to look forward to, and when he wants to share something beautiful that he's created, Chef likes to invite a few guests to have dinner here at the on-site kitchen of the Chameleon Fox. The menu is always a surprise, and is often inspired by his daily trips to the local food market. He spends about an hour and a half each morning casually strolling down each of the aisles in his now perfected pattern; spices and dried goods first, followed by the aromatic herbs, fruits and vegetables, ending with fish, beef and poultry. I've watched as he's become instantly inspired by walking past a nearly overflowing basket of sunburst colored squash blossoms. The bright gradient orange and yellows contrasted by their sage green stems stopped him in his tracks, and immediately piqued his interest. So much so that he purchased enough blossoms to fill two grocery sacks. That quick moment sparked a creative firestorm that resulted in a menu option that he called "Squash Blossoms in Bloom". The flowers were prepared three ways; stuffed with halloumi and goat cheeses and fried, sauteed in Irish butter and garlic, and lastly roasted with Swiss chard and ricotta cheese. Guests that were staying at the Chameleon Fox that night raved about the plate for days, and wrote reviews praising the innovation of the plate, and how they were still thinking about the meal weeks after they had checked out of their villas. Responses like that push him to create other dishes that leave his guests with the insatiable feeling of wanting one more bite, coupled with the finality of knowing that they'll never taste anything else like it again in their lifetime. It's a perpetual cycle of explosive inspiration and creativity, commanding his guests to call each of their senses into the present moment while they are fully submerged in the experience. A reminder that time is both precious and fleeting, euphoric and quickly dissolving, and that we cannot be in such a rush to move through the present to get to the future. Or else we run the risk of missing the sweetness of the now.

The Chameleon Fox is a bed and breakfast camouflaged amongst the Costa Rican jungles, and the outward representation of Chef's introverted nature. He wanted the property to serve as a hideaway for guests that want to experience the relaxation and anonymity that comes with being on vacation. Staff members move quietly about the property, discreetly anticipating the needs of guests. For the most part, Chef is a private person and keeps to himself when he isn't working. A residual habit that he picked up from working odd hours, that aligned with his already introverted nature. Since moving here, he's created a life of balance between the work and the personal, intentionally keeping the two parts separate. He's kind and personable with the neighbors and his staff, and has made some great friends here over the last few years. He enjoys going out and exploring the city when he has the time, but if given the choice, he would prefer to stay home and enjoy the fruits of his nearly ten year labor. He appreciates simple pleasures like a glass or two of Cabernet Sauvignon in the afternoon with lunch, and marathon games of League of Legends that begin at the end of his work day and don't end until the sun comes up. While he's an incredibly gracious host, he hasn't had a dinner party at his home since moving in, so tonight is a very rare occasion. He's invited some friends and family for a dinner party that he's been planning for a few weeks, and I can't help but wonder about the timing. We've been settled into the house for about a year and half now, and not once has he mentioned throwing a party here. Considering his natural gravitation to seclusion, and the lengthy process of getting the house and all of it's details exactly the way he wanted, I assumed he wanted us to keep the house to ourselves for a bit longer before inviting guests. Which gives me reason to question if there might be another reason behind his invitations.

I woke up this morning smiling at a text from him with a photo of some gorgeous filet mignons and other vegetables I couldn't identify in a shopping cart from his early morning grocery store haul. I can't help but to be excited when he sends messages like that, because I know it will lead to the creation of something out of this world. Hiis mind works in ways I've never experienced in anyone else. He's the kind of guy you notice in a crowd, but not for the reasons you might think. Aside from his 6'4 stature, his deep voice and laugh that can fill a room, he's incredibly introspective and forward thinking. I like when he describes something that he's eaten and enjoyed, he says it's "really tasty" instead of just "good", and he doesn't like anything on top of his steak because, as he so eloquently puts it, "if you need to offer people something to put on top of your steak, then what the fuck is wrong with your steak?". He likes slow mornings that are spent with a blunt or two, a steaming cup of turmeric and ginger tea, and lo-fi beats. On the rare occasion he doesn't have to be in the kitchen until later in the day, he'll make eggs, toast and tea and we'll spend time swapping stories while listening to Prince. There's always an open window, the semi-sweet scent of burning incense, and a soft purple glow coming from the aquaponics tank for herbs and vegetables.

The Chameleon Fox started out as a concept in Chef's imagination when he was in his early twenties. He dreamed of owning and operating a unique vacation destination where he could prepare dishes that challenged the culinary rules that he was taught in school.   Finding the perfect plot of land was paramount to everything else, considering that he wanted to use two or three acres for vegetable gardens and orchards for fruit trees. For Chef, preparing food that he's grown himself is incredibly fulfilling. He would always tell me that "it's really important to know where your food comes from, and to know that it's not contaminated with bullshit". The Western way is to genetically modify food against pesticides in effort to produce enough to feed the masses, but always at the expense of nutritional value and taste. So Chef made it a point to study variations of seeds with the goal of figuring out how to modify the taste of the produce without the use of chemicals. Once we found an area that had rich, nutrient dense soil that could produce healthy vegetation, he got to work drawing up the blueprints for the bed and breakfast units. He spent ten frustrating months interviewing, hiring and firing four different architects before finding the perfect team that clearly understood his vision. Nick and Terry, two laid back older guys from Austin, Texas came out of retirement to help bring Chef's plans to life. They had several meetings with Chef at Nick's home office to nail down specifics like the amount of sunlight that each guest unit would get at different times of day, and the most ideal places to watch the sunset. Each of those meetings ended with a joint and special reserve bourbon to celebrate their progress and toast to what was to come.

After purchasing the land, the first thing Chef did was meet with some of the local farmers and hire staff to plant the garden and set up a state of the art irrigation system around the property. Chef had already procured seeds from all over the world for the garden, like Swiss chard, red leaf lettuce, collards, purple stripe garlic, black beans, and a variety of carrots and herbs. The staff meticulously carved out forty rows in the garden plot and planted the seeds with enough space between them to allow room for the harvest. The orchard was planted a few feet away from the garden rows, and would later give life to perfectly ripe figs, avocados, and the juiciest nectarines I've ever had. Looking back, the process seemed much shorter than it actually was. Probably because of how many trips we took back and forth from Houston to San Jose, and being able to watch the progress happen a few months at a time.

For me, the best part about visiting the property was the initial drive toward the entrance. Nick and Terry thought that it was important for them to design the property from the perspective of the guests as they would arrive. Chef took their suggestion to heart, and insisted that the guests felt like they were ensconced in an ethereal dreamworld from the moment they left the main road. He worked closely with the staff to carefully plant and place trees and lush ground covering along both sides of the mile-long driveway. Now, monstrous trees with outstretched branches and low sweeping vines provide a deep green shade, and the songs of birds and crawling creatures welcome the guests to their temporary home. Each of the three bungalow-style guest houses are separated by soursop and passionfruit trees and a winding walking trail, where guests can explore the jungle and all of the creatures that call it home. The houses were designed to have open concept living spaces with chestnut hardwood flooring throughout. They each have one bedroom with a king sized bed facing wide French doors that open up to a private balcony and twelve foot wide swimming pool. Majestic trees and vines surround the pool and deck area, making the guests feel immersed in their own piece of paradise. Each villa has a small kitchen, but they are rarely used because of the elaborate room service delivered by the staff. During their stay, guests are provided with breakfast, lunch, dinner, and a heavy appetizer course based on the signature Chef Kababo menu. A collection of nearly one hundred recipes that Chef developed and perfected from his time in Europe, and from his years of cooking in Houston as an Executive Chef.

The menu includes some of my personal favorite options: ribeye with roasted duck fat potatoes and sauteed Swiss chard with blistered tomatoes and mushrooms, and the smoked chicken leg quarters with creamed spinach and cauliflower rice that actually tastes like fluffy rice and not crunchy cauliflower.

Today started out like a normal Tuesday for Chef. An early morning trip to the grocery store to get fresh produce for the kitchen and the day's menu, and handling administrative things. But for the people that are invited for this evening's feast, they'll leave with something more than just a full belly and satisfied appetite. They'll get to take a piece of his story.

Chapter 2

Pawn to E4

As a chef, there's nothing like walking into a really clean kitchen. I realized that everyone has a different definition of cleanliness when I first started my apprenticeship in France. The kitchens that I worked in were so pristine. I couldn't believe that people actually worked in them because they looked like some sort of studio model home setup. They used a water hose to spray under the stoves and prep tables, and followed up with sweeping, brushing, squeegeeing & mopping the floor, after every service, each day. That's when I realized that my version of cleanliness was actually dirty.
– Kababo

It's right around noon, and I can feel my eyes getting tired from staring at my computer. For the last few weeks, I've been working on a proposal for my second book and it's taken up most of my time during the day while Kababo works in the main kitchen on the property. The first book was surprisingly successful, and I had only written and released it with the intention of getting out of my head and getting over the fear of accomplishing what I've always wanted to do. I've been a writer for as long as I can remember, and when I was a kid, I would make up stories about far away places, and little girls with glasses and superpowers. In high school, I wrote for the Journalism Club, and followed the "high school newspaper journalist to major publication intern" pipeline. I had dreams of writing my own books, but other projects (and excuses) always seemed to get in the way. When Chef and I first met and I told him about wanting to write, he casually pointed out that my procrastination was a form of self-sabotage, because beneath the surface I was afraid of the success that might come from it, and what people would think about my work. I was stunned by his candor, but appreciated the honesty. He told me to start writing in spite of the fear, because in his mind, fear is only a construct meant to immobilize its victims. He was absolutely right.

I tried to ignore my tired eyes and write a few more paragraphs, but rumbling hunger pangs let me know it was time to take a break. This is my favorite time of the day; when the afternoon sunlight comes through the windows at just the right angle illuminating the plants and their trailing leaves in the window sills. It's one of the many simple pleasures that I've come to appreciate and be thankful for in our new home. Others include the walks that Chef and I take together through the property on Sunday mornings. He'll usually wake up before me to fill his travel cup with hot herbal tea, and mine with sweet and creamy coffee. Then we start on the two mile walk, spotting wild Birds of Paradise plants and pointing out the animals and exotic birds that at one time, we could only see at the Houston Zoo back home.

I walked into the kitchen to take out some cheese and crackers for a little midday snack, when I heard the heavy back door slam shut and the triple beep from the security alarm. Just then, his deep voice came rumbling towards me. "Tonight, we feast like kings!" he said in a playful melodramatic voice with his arms outstretched. He's got a mischievous look about him today, like he's got a secret plan that he's just waiting to watch unfold. I smiled at him and watched as he hoisted the reusable grocery bags onto the countertop next to me, preparing to proudly show me the spoils from his successful trip to the markets, like he does every morning. "Harissa, scotch bonnets, fresh lump crab, whole wheat flour, vanilla bean pods, fresh eggs, and some other shit that's not your business!" he said with a smile as he quickly turned his back toward me and scurried to the massive refrigerator, trying to keep his secret treasures to himself. "Excuse you!" I said. I walked over to the refrigerator and tried to stretch my five foot, seven inch frame over his shoulder to see what he had put away. "Let me see it!" I begged playfully, knowing full well that this would get me nowhere. "Mind your business!" This cat and mouse game has been ongoing for years now. Him and his super secret recipes and ingredients, and me with an insatiable curiosity about how he turns the most interesting things into eccentric dishes fit for a five star restaurant.

I accepted my defeat and went back to the countertop, taking what I assumed to be some kind of turnip from one of the grocery bags and held it up to my nose. As if smelling it would somehow help me to classify it. "And what exactly do you plan on doing with all of this tonight, Chef Kababo?". He took the mystery vegetable from my hand, smiled and winked at me then turned around to continue putting the groceries away. A response like that from him meant that I would find out the menu when the time came. I let out an exaggerated "fine" over my shoulder, and made my way back to my laptop to get some more work done. "It's kohlrabi", he yelled to me, and I couldn't help but laugh.

A few minutes later as I was searching for a playlist to help me get through the next few hours of work, I looked up to see him set a plate of snacks on the matte black lap tray next to me before he walked away. He's added some sliced meats that he must have picked up from the store this morning, kalamata olives, nuts, grapes and nectarine slices. Somehow, he elevated my measly snack into something of beauty. He's

constantly bringing me a plate of food, or having me taste an element of a dish that he's

made. Not because he's looking for my approval, but because he knows just how much

I love food and that these small bites always make me smile.

As a kid, I would come home after school and make salads for myself, finding joy

in chopping and slicing the vegetables, and experimenting with different vinegars and

oils for the dressing. My parents worked late, so Ina Garten and Nigella Lawson

welcomed me home every day with beautiful meals. Watching them move about their

television kitchens made me long for my own space, where I could play and create and

make delicious things that were just for me. Fast forward to when I moved into my first

apartment, and Pinterest had taken the world by storm, I experimented with recipes that

my family would never have been open to trying. A lavender pound cake or a chilled

creamy basil soup would have gone unappreciated, but I relished in the experience.

When I had the opportunity to move to Houston, David Chang's documentary Ugly

Delicious had just been released on Netflix, and I was elated at the thought of living in a

city that was known for some of the most diverse and incredible food in the U.S. When I

got there, I made it a point to try out as many places as I could even if I didn't have

anyone to go with.

Enter Kababo. We met at Izakaya, one of my favorite Japanese restaurants in

midtown, and I'll never forget it. It was lunch time, and I was sitting in the crowded

dining area next to a window with a magazine. I was casually flipping through the pages between bites of yellowtail and garlic edamame when I saw him walk through the door. I noticed his height initially, but what caught my attention was the way he held the door open for a mother who was trying to corral her two small children out of the restaurant. I watched as he smiled at her and said something that must have been reassuring, because she smiled back and let out a heavy sigh of gratitude. I went back to my magazine, but couldn't help but look for him. He sat two or three tables away from me, and our eyes met a couple of times before we exchanged polite smiles. The waiter brought my cucumber salad and kimchi ramen to the table, when I heard his voice say "Excuse me, I don't mean to bother you, but what is that? It looks amazing." I smiled, happy that he had broken the ice. I told him what it was and that it was my favorite and he asked if I was a regular. I told him that it was one of the best lunch spots in the area, and that it was one of the few places that I had been to in Houston that gave me some comfort after moving from California. "Really?", he asked with his right eyebrow raised in intrigue. I told him all about my beloved hometown, how I had gotten too comfortable there, and how I knew I needed to leave to get to the next phase of my life. I asked what he did for work and he told me he was a chef and the next thing I knew, we were talking about documentaries, local restaurants, and weird trends in food. He had devoured his sashimi by that point, and said that he had to get back to the kitchen but would love to continue our conversation over dinner. We exchanged phone numbers and he promised to give me a call later with details. He called, we ate, and we've been eating together ever since.

At the height of his career in Houston, his two bedroom apartment doubled as an office space, and oftentimes a storage unit for his catering supplies and kitchen equipment. Boxes of chafing dishes and industrial sized coffee makers sat in the living room, sharing the space with a pull out couch that he slept on. His intention was to work hard for the duration of the lease and save his money, so he didn't want the apartment to be too comfortable. His mind was always racing and thinking three steps ahead of his staff, and the only time he cooked was when he had to. Almost never for leisure and very rarely, if ever, for me. I had to damn near beg for him to make me a grilled cheese sandwich, my all-time favorite late night snack, but I understood why cooking took so much out of him at the time. He truly has a love and deep respect for the art of culinary. The idea of creating something delicious from scratch, and seeing it through each stage, from garden to cutting board, to pan and to plate has always excited him. He always says watching people take in each bite and seeing their face change to express what they're experiencing from the food is what makes it all worth it to him. It's why he went to culinary school in the first place, and what has afforded him the life that he lives so fully now. But running such a demanding and fast-paced business like he did back then left him very little room to exist and be free in that creative space, and very little energy to cook for himself at all. There were many times when our conversations about food would lead him to confess that he had Whataburger or breakfast food for dinner, because he just didn't have it in him to cook. His lack of groceries could have also been at fault for that though. For the most part, his refrigerator was bare except for the few condiments in the door compartment, leftover takeout containers, and maybe a carton of eggs. Things are much different now though. Now, he cooks whenever he feels like it and always has something delicious tucked away in a silver two-quart container secured with cling wrap; a habit from his restaurant days that stuck with him.

"Look at this!', Chef said as he walked back into the living room with the latest issue of Bon Appetit magazine in his hands. It was the latest food review from the one and only Antonio Cardenas, former chef turned renowned food writer, and Chef's number one critic. He's written reviews on several of Chef's operations back in Houston, and each review was more harsh than the one before it. Mr. Cardenas' overall attitude toward Chef's food was that it's mediocre and lacks vision, and it always drove Chef crazy. Not because he's being criticized harshly, but because he feels it's unfair. While Houston is known for being a cultural melting pot, and the food mecca of the United States, a lot chefs have a difficult time getting fresh produce and high quality ingredients. This is likely the reason why there aren't any Michelin star restaurants in Texas, despite being known for having hundreds of restaurants and food joints within a 5 mile radius. It's not for lack of talented chefs or patrons willing to support, but Texas doesn't have the same opportunities for fresh ingredients like New York or California. When it came to going head to head with Cardenas, Chef felt like the odds were always against him, like playing carnival games for hours, only to realize he'd never win. What I never understood about their relationship was the way Cardenas almost seemed to take pleasure out of writing the things he said about Chef, and how despite Chef never caring about what anyone else had to say about his food, he was hell bent on getting Cardenas to see his food for what it was. I also never understood why Cardenas seemed to follow Chef throughout his culinary career. When Chef finished culinary school in 2014 and was working in Europe, Cardenas caught wind of Chef's glowing reputation from his mentors and showed up on a busy night to the restaurant where he was working. Chef remembers it vividly, and tells the story often.

"He saw me from the dining room and immediately knew who I was, because all the other chefs and staff were French guys, and I'm this tall ass light skinned brotha so it wasn't hard for him to find me. We made eye contact, and there was something that I recognized about him that I didn't like, but I couldn't figure it out and that should've been my first clue. I didn't know he was a food critic, but I knew he wasn't just a regular patron or a tourist coming in for a Michelin star meal. He carried himself differently than the other people that we served, and I could smell his arrogance from the moment he walked in. He ordered the Beef Bourguignon and I remember thinking that he was about to be pleasantly surprised, because the head chef and I had nailed that recipe down weeks ago and it was perfect. It was fucking delicious. Everybody loved it, and I loved preparing it. I watched as the server took the order out to him, and noticed that he already had a near-empty glass of white wine at his table. Who orders white wine with a beef dish? That's not how it goes. Everyone knows that white wine is for lighter dishes like fish or pasta with a white sauce or something like that. And if they don't know, a guy like that definitely would have known. Fast forward two weeks, and this asshole writes a review about how the plate lacked depth and the flavor was mediocre. Then wrote this condescending ass line about how the Head Chef should keep a closer eye on the newest chef on his team."

Cardenas' latest review was written six months ago during his trip to Houston when he stopped by Chef's restaurant. Chef was in town to visit some family and tie up some loose ends, so he planned to be in the kitchen that night. Chef said he spotted him walking into the dining room from where he was standing in the kitchen, just like the first time and several times after, and as usual, he immediately knew that whatever he was going to write was going to be unfair. We still can't figure out how Cardenas even knew that Chef would be in town, especially since we had made the move to Costa Rica. But somehow he knew, and showed up on the one night that Chef was running the kitchen.

"I don't want to say that he has it out for me or anything," Chef said as he sat down next to me. "But I've read what he's written about other chefs in Houston, and he's tough on them too but their reviews aren't nearly as critical as mine. This dude dissects every single dish that we serve him down to the tiniest particle, and holds it to a damn near-impossible standard." "Why do you think he keeps coming back to eat your food if he critiques it so unfairly?" I asked as I took a bite of sharp cheddar cheese and salami. "That's what I've been trying to figure out for years! This dude has followed my whole professional career, and not once has he written about my food in a positive light. Not once! I can't stand him. I don't understand him." He let out a deep exhale and stretched his long legs out in front of him, and crossed his arms in front of his chest. "Read it to me," he asked, and of course I obliged.

"In March of 2019, I had the pleasure of spending time with friends in one of my favorite cities, Houston, Texas. Houston is vibrant, full of life, and bursting with culture that is effortlessly reflected in the food. Every time I'm able to make a trip to the city, I always try to squeeze in a little work (and a lot of eating), and for this trip I was able to eat at Touch Of Sirius, where Texas born and bred bad boy chef himself, Kababo, is the Executive Chef. I first encountered Chef Kababo in Vendee France a few years ago, when he was working under Michelin Guide Chef David Nicolas at Labata St.Thomas. My initial critique highlighted his food as being mediocre and how Chef David Nicolas should keep a closer eye on him, so with this most recent trip to Houston, I wanted to check in and see what role time and experience in the kitchen played in his culinary skills. Much to my disappointment, there was very little growth, if any. For my entree, a stuffed chicken marsala with whipped potatoes and crème *fraiche and vegetables. Upon ordering, I assumed that since I had selected such a classic dish, my previous experience with Chef Kababo's food could be a distant memory and this would be his redemption song. However, in this instance I somehow let my high hopes distract me from the old adage that reminds us of what happens when we assume. The dish was awful. The chicken was overly seasoned but cooked well - this was perhaps the only bright spot of the plate. The vegetables were limp, dull in color and taste which can only lead me to believe that he used what he had available to him - scraps.*

I've always been vocal about the quality of a dish being based on the quality of the ingredients, and I think that may have been the demise of the dish. As I mentioned, Chef Kababo is located in Houston, Texas, a port city known for its rich cultural diversity that is reflected in the gastronomy. Located on the Gulf Coast, the Port of Houston is one of the largest ports in the United States. An incredible feat to the credit of the city, but a major detriment to those who work in fine dining. Unlike chefs on the East and West Coast of the U.S., chefs in Texas do not have access to high quality ingredients. They have to use produce and other ingredients that have traveled far and wide to get to them, with the quality diminishing with each transport. Despite the lack of top quality produce, there are quite literally hundreds, if not thousands of restaurants in Houston alone. Although many fail to remain operational after two to three years because, in my opinion, there are just too many places to eat. Nevertheless, Chef Kababo has been able to maintain his reputation as one of Houston's hottest chefs despite his mediocre menus and abandonment of culinary tradition. Perhaps his patrons are accustomed to eating dishes made with bad produce. Or maybe the standard for professional culinary arts is far too low, and has sadly become the norm. Whatever the reason, my hope is that Chef Kababo is able to overcome this seemingly insurmountable problem of being geographically bound to low quality ingredients, and somehow, in some way, figures out to simply make better food. "

Chef let out a heavy sigh and shook his head as he took the magazine from my hands. It's the same reaction he always has to something Cardenas has written; half annoyance and half disappointment. "I wonder how a conversation would go with him?", I asked. "I can't imagine a guy like that would be opposed to having a conversation to elaborate on his opinions, especially since they're so strong." "We've talked! That's also what drives me crazy. Even though he comes across as an asshole in his reviews, he's actually a pretty decent guy. He knows about my culinary training, and the time I spent overseas training with my mentors, and he's talked to me about his opinions on the regional differences in Texas food versus the more upscale style of food on the West and East Coast. He definitely knows his shit, and from what I've heard he does his thing in the kitchen too. Dude understands food, and knows great food when it's in front of him." He was stroking at his long beard as he spoke, which let me know he was deep in thought and had been thinking about the whole ordeal for quite some time now. "I'm not an arrogant guy most days," he started. "But I know that my food is amazing and I can cook my ass off. That much I know. So I know there's something that he likes about my food that keeps him coming back. I don't know if it's a Jedi mind trick, reverse psychology, Mr. Miyagi thing or what. But it gets under my skin". "I think he's obsessed with you," I said flatly, looking him square in the face and meaning every word I said. "Obsessed?" His right eyebrow was raised almost to the top of his forehead, the way it always is when he's appalled or confused by something. "Obsessed! Why else would he be so focused on your career? All these other chefs and reviews that he's written, not once has he written about the same chef more than once. He's written twice about you."

I said. "Why you? Why didn't he write about you the first time, and then be done with it? There's something there, I'm telling you."

       I've always thought this about Cardenas, but never brought it to Chef's attention because I wasn't sure if it was just in my head. But it wasn't. Cardenas was notorious for going to a restaurant, ripping it to shreds in a review, and never going back or giving the chef an opportunity for redemption. But I also think, to some degree, that Chef was a little obsessed with Cardenas himself. Not with him as a person, but with coming to understand him and why he operated the way he did. Every time a new food review came out, Chef had to read it. Returning home from the grocery store with the latest issue of the magazine tucked into his bags before sitting at the kitchen table reading it with me, and then taking it with him to the main kitchen of Chameleon Fox and dissecting it with his team. For whatever reason, Chef was just as interested in getting inside the mind of his nemesis.

       "I don't know, B. I don't care about what he says. You know I don't put a lot of stock in what people say about me or my food." It's true. He really didn't. "Especially if they don't have the credentials to comment or critique my food. But he actually knows what he's talking about, so I don't understand why he's always on my case," he said. "I'm telling you! It's an obsession. He's fascinated by you, and can't stand it so he wants to keep you close by writing these reviews that he knows is going to drive you insane. That's why he keeps popping up like that! To keep you on your toes and to keep his hooks in you."

"Well, maybe we'll figure it out tonight," he said as he stood up from his seat. "What do you mean, tonight?" I asked. "You invited him to the house?" "Yep!" he hollered as he was already on his way to the kitchen. I couldn't believe it. Critics from all over the world have written about him and his food; most of them raving about his innovation and him being the next 'whoever their favorite chef is'. And never once has he thought twice about who the critics were or the basis of their review. Except for Cardenas. And tonight, he'll be here in the flesh. I couldn't get over it. "Why would you want him to come tonight?" I asked as I followed him into the kitchen. "Because I want him to see me in my element, and on my terms. I want him to experience my food the way that I've always intended it to be enjoyed." Typical Kababo. Once his mind was set on something, it was a done deal. Cemented and unmovable. All I could do in the moment was nod my head, because I knew he was right. Cardenas has always had it out for Chef. Or so it seemed. And tonight would be the reckoning.

Chapter 3

Filet Mignon Egg Rolls

I've always been the "I can do anything" type of person, often to my own foolery. I had to be 10 years old when I was cooking dinner for my grandparents. Some chicken and pasta with sauce type of thing, nothing major but I wanted to show them I could do it. Always seeing both my grandfather & father move swiftly with the blade I attempted to do the same thing, in all of my arragorance. It goes without saying I sliced a very large chunk of my left index finger about 90% off, and what did my 10 yr old self do? Went to the bathroom and with my grandfather's nail clipper kit, I proceeded to remove the hanging flap of skin that was keeping this chunk of finger attached. I wrapped it up, finished the dinner, and never said a thing about my finger. If my 10yr old child had an injury to their hand like that and didn't tell me I would be so furious with them.
–Kababo

Hours have passed, and all that's left of my midday mini charcuterie plate are the discarded bitter bits of fruit and pistachio shells. The grandfather clock in the corner chimes, marking the five o'clock hour just as I responded to the last email from my literary agent. Chef is moving around in the kitchen with an uptempo playlist blasting on his speaker. "Outstanding" by The GAP Band started to play, so I took that as my cue to go check on things. He's got a folded hand towel hanging from the front pocket of his apron and a pen tucked behind his ear. His long arms skillfully toss the contents of the screaming hot pan into the air and catch them again with a sizzle. He's completely focused, but still hitting all the high notes in the chorus. Whenever he's home and in the mood to cook, which is a rarity, I love to watch the process. It's like watching a master conductor skillfully direct an orchestra through a complicated piece of music. "Smells good!" I shouted to him from the entryway of the kitchen. Without saying a word to me, he tore off a piece of crusty sourdough bread from a loaf on the countertop, generously dipped it into a saucepan and handed it to me. He leaned back against the countertop and wiped the sweat from his brow, watching as I brought the bite to my lips. My eyes grew wide and my face immediately lit up. I savored the bite and it's sauce, and was a little sad when the last of the morsel was swallowed. He knew it was good, and smiled at me with pride.

Seeing him like this, happy and taking command of the kitchen, reminds me a bit of his Houston Meal Prep days. Only this time, he doesn't have a team to help him prepare and cook tonight's meal. He wants to do this one himself. He could easily call Lucas, his protege and right hand man during the week, but for some reason he's set on cooking the entire meal by himself. Although I'm sure Lucas will be standing at the ready in case Chef needs him to help out with anything.

The music is interrupted by an incoming call on his cellphone. "Hey, what's going on?....Are you serious?... How the fuck did you do that?" I can tell right away that it was Tory on the other end. He starts to laugh and shake his head, which is his usual response when his little brother does typical little brother things. "Man, what time is the next connecting flight?... Alright that should still get you here at a decent time. Let me know if anything changes...Alright, yeah the driver will be waiting outside the baggage claim... Okay cool, bye." The ending of the song comes back at full blast and Chef looks at me with a deadpan look on his face. "I don't know how you miss a flight when you live fifteen minutes away from the airport, but Tory made it happen" he said as he turned his attention back to the stove.

Tory is the epitome of a 21 year old kid. Loves to hang out with his friends and spend money he doesn't have to impress his social media followers, and gets girls by making them "fancy" meals that his big brother taught him. He's forgetful, but kind. A little absentminded at times, but he's got a good heart and really looks up to Chef. I have a soft spot for him because he reminds me a lot of my younger brother back home in California, and being a big sister is one of my favorite things to be.
"He'll get here just in time for dinner if his flight lands on time," he hollers to me over the music.

The entire house smells incredible, and I don't know if I'll be able to wait to eat until dinner starts and guests arrive. In an effort to distract myself, I stepped out into the backyard to help with the setup for the evening. Bright, glittering bouquets of orange and pink flowers lay scattered on the white linen covered tables, and I can already tell they'll be the perfect accents to tonight's spread. Chef's arranged for his favorite local florist and friend Miguel Quesada, to send over a few regionally grown flowers from his florist shop to use for decoration before he and his wife arrive, but from the looks of it he threw in a lot extra. They've worked together on a few events, and have become fast friends. Bonded over their shared love of good food and video games.

Initially, I was nervous about the way he might be perceived here. He was a Black man from the U.S. who only spoke broken "kitchen Spanish", and wanted to break ground to build a completely unique bed and breakfast. But he never flinched, and made it work. He made it a point to introduce himself to the neighbors, and to let them know that he respected the area and wanted to be a part of the community. He hosted small dinners for a few families in the area, and they all welcomed him with open arms, happily sharing their food and culture with him. Now the neighbors regularly bring him produce from their gardens, and homemade dishes and treats to express their love and appreciation, and he gladly reciprocates.

The backyard tablescapes are almost set, and I walk over to see Dani putting her finishing touch on the decor. She's Chef's second-in-command at the Chameleon Fox, and Lucas' older sister. Dani is probably the only person that he would trust with his vision for tonight. She's 25 years old with a bold confidence that I've never seen in anyone her age, and wears her long brown hair in a tight military-style bun that projects her no nonsense attitude.

"Hola, B!" she said, as she dusted glitter from her hands and straightened her crisp white button down shirt. "It looks good right?". "It's beautiful! You did a great job, and he's going to love it" I reassured her. "Good, that's exactly what I want." She touched my arm and motioned for me to come toward her. "He's kind of going all out for this party, no? Even the parties that we have for the bed and breakfast guests aren't this nice. What's going on?", she asked. I had been wondering the same thing, but didn't have an answer. "I honestly don't know," I said. "But I'm thinking we all might need to be ready for anything." She looked at me with raised eyebrows and nodded her head before her attention shifted to Lucas. He walked into the backyard from the side gate, carrying boxes of drinkware stacked so high that he couldn't quite see over them. "Hey! Be careful with that," she hollered at her brother. "You're going to break them, and I know your broke ass doesn't have any money to replace them." Dani excused herself from our conversation and she ran over to help him get things situated.

Just then, Chef and his serving team began filing in and out of the kitchen to the backyard carrying a chafing dish and plates. The sun was beginning to set as the rhythmic beats of Samba music filled the backyard, and the temperature dropped to a breezy 65 degrees. It's a perfect evening to spend near the fire pit, sipping something strong and delicious while enjoying conversation with interesting people. The spacious yard was accentuated by delicately placed string lights along the pergola that illuminated the deck. But the main source of light tonight is the glow coming from the fire pit. Tall flames seated in the deep bowl of the pit, giving a warm and welcoming light to the yard. By it, I can see some familiar faces begin to enter the backyard. Everyone here, in some way, has a connection to Chef.

Not surprisingly, Miguel and Paola Quesada are the first to arrive and from what I can see, they're already arguing. Paola mumbled something in Spanglish about him not trusting her directions, and he snapped back at her saying that she doesn't respect him. I've heard them argue over less. They are a fascinating couple, and their presence at any gathering is always unforgettable. Miguel is a third generation florist and Costa Rica native, and he knows almost everything there is to know about horticulture and the florist business. He's a pretentious know-it-all but means well, and he's the kind of person that always remembers tiny details about you and will always have your back. Paola is brilliant, strikingly beautiful, and always commands attention whenever she enters a room. She was a very successful model in the 90s; print ads and commercials mostly. But she gave it up to pursue degrees in International Relations and Gender Studies, and now guest lectures at the university. She comes from money, and her parents hate that she chose to marry Miguel when she could have had a substantially better life with someone of a more reputable background, and they never let her forget it. She and Miguel never agree on anything and are known for having abrupt arguments at any time and in front of anyone. They're also known for sneaking away during any type of gathering to have sex, then returning to their guests as if nothing has happened. I think it's a toxic relationship, and the way they fight can't possibly be healthy. Chef says it's the fire between them that makes their relationship work so well. He appreciates passion in any form, and doesn't seem to be bothered by Paola and Miguel's outbursts or sexual expression. He just lets them be themselves.

"That's enough," Paola says sharply, lowering her voice and quickly pulling her arm away from Miguel to remove herself from the discussion. She knew that starting an argument with him on their way to the party would spark frustration in Miguel. Not so much that he would truly be upset with her, but just enough to cause him to run his hand up the back of her nape and grab a fistful of her hair as he whispered his love for her in her ear. That was how she liked it. Miguel spotted me from across the yard, and waved me over. "There she is!", he said, embracing me and planting a kiss on both of my cheeks. He held out his hands for me to hold so that he could get a good look at me, the way he always does. "How's it been going over here today?," he asks. He knows that Chef can put a lot of pressure on himself when it comes to details because he wants everything to be excellent. "It's actually been really good. He's focused but there's a lightness about him today which is always nice to see," I said as we both turned toward the house to see Chef giving his team their marching orders for the evening. Paola returned from the bar with her usual captivating grin and two glasses of champagne. "Well there she is! Look at you, pretty!", she said as she hugged me. She handed one of the glasses to me and sipped on the other. Intentional. Miguel was clearly surprised that she didn't bring a drink for him, and Paola gave no attention to the matter. "Paola! I'm so glad you two were able to make it!" I said. "I know! It's so good to see you, it's been too long! You'll have to come to the house for dinner soon", she said. In addition to her fiery personality, Paola can cook her ass off and loves to show off for an audience; and Chef and I are always willing and excited to volunteer.

I like to watch people, and see how they interact with others in certain social settings. Tonight, I see friends and family standing together, laughing about things that happened the last time they got together. Everyone here knows and is connected to Chef in some way, but most of them are strangers to each other and meeting for the first time tonight. Whatever the draw, and for whatever reason, they are a part of his world and have the benefit of experiencing some of his most delicious creations whenever he calls.

By now, most of the group has made their way over to the appetizers that lay on top of a table that can't be classified as anything other than art. Chef prepared a beautiful buffet spread adorned with the tropical flowers that arrived earlier in the day, courtesy of Miguel and his flower shop, and an impressive display of charcuterie and fruit carvings. At the center of the table is the obvious center of attention; a large golden pyramid shaped chafing dish filled with his signature filet mignon egg rolls. It's a pleasure to watch people fall in love with his food just as quickly as I did. The egg rolls are otherworldly, and everyone that has at least one on their plate is trying their best to make sense of them with each taste. That's the thing about good food - once you've had a bite of something incredible, you savor it by taking in more.

I've watched Chef make these egg rolls probably a dozen times, and I still don't know the full recipe. I know that he uses the best filet mignon that he can find, adds a mixture of aromatic spices that he grinds himself, and something else that I taste but can't identify, then wraps and lightly fries them before cutting each one. When he plates them, he spoons his famous Horseradish Dijon Aioli on the base of the plate. It sounds so simple when I put it like that, but I promise the description doesn't do the process justice.

Between bites and catching clips of conversations around me, I glanced over at the sliding glass door that leads inside the house to see Chef stepping outside from the kitchen. He's dressed casually, no chef whites tonight. Only Creative Recreations sneakers, olive green pants and a chambray button up with the sleeves cuffed right at the elbow revealing his tattoos. There's a look of contentment and pride on his face as he stepped onto the grass. His 15 year old daughter, Kamryn, walked over to him with an eggroll in her hand. She leaned into his side as he put his arm around her and looked at what she was eating. She's the spitting image of Chef, and every bit as kind and curious as he is. Petite and spritely, with tailbone length knotless box braids, and a bright smile, recently emancipated after two years in braces. Chef has tried to spark an interest in her for culinary, but it never took. She prefers reading, art and video games over being in the kitchen, although she's inevitably learned some of his tricks. One night last summer, Chef and I were sitting in the family room playing Uno and having wine when we heard some rumbling in the kitchen. We walked over and saw Kamryn standing in the kitchen, wearing one of her dad's old t-shirts while plating a perfect golden brown croque madame that she made for a midnight snack. Chef was floored. I was sure he would be concerned about her being awake that late, but instead he was impressed that she made such an elevated dish on her own. She just looked at him blankly, shrugged and said "I was hungry" before taking a bite and walking back to her room.

I looked over at him and saw that he was almost beaming as he greeted his friends, and welcomed everyone to the party. Making it a point to individually connect and make eye contact with everyone there. For him, aside from all of the notability and assumed prestige that comes with his profession, it truly is a pleasure for him to have them there.

While he was in a conversation with Miguel, our eyes met and we exchanged smiles, indicative of a few things all at once: how cool it is that we're actually standing in the backyard of his dream home in another country, that he likely made something tonight that he knows will trigger a pleasant memory for me, and the promise of connecting later tonight.

The conversations in the crowd soften as he steps onto the deck, and raises his long arms above his head to signal that he has something to say. "I want to thank you all for coming out tonight and allowing me the honor of cooking for you. Tonight, I have prepared some lovely dishes, but some of you won't be surprised by that. So I ask that you have an open mind, and that you try to expand your palette a little bit this evening. With that, ya'll come on into the house, and let's eat!"

The chatter sparks up again with a thrill of excitement in the air, sort of like when you've been standing in line for a rollercoaster for about an hour, and it's finally your turn to get on. Some guests are quickly taking in their last few bites of filet mignon egg rolls, while others go back for seconds and thirds before we enter the house.

Chef was holding his cell phone in his hand and pulled me to the side, out of earshot from the rest of the guests. "He's here," he said. "Who? Cardenas?" I asked. "Yep. He just called and said that he was lost and couldn't find the house. Do you mind taking one of the golf carts to go get him?" I think he could tell by the look on my face that I wasn't excited about the task, but he knew I was up for it. "Sure, I'll be back in a little bit."

I followed the cement pavers in the backyard to the side of the house where the three golf carts are lined up. The property isn't overwhelmingly large, but it can be a bit much to go from one end to the other on foot, so we figured the carts would be perfect.

I walked over to the keypad and entered the code to open the automatic gate, and started up the first cart in line. The drive from the house to the front of the property is always stunning at any time of day, but tonight there was something magical about it. I hear the excited playful screams of the neighborhood kids in the distance as they play soccer in the nearby fields and it brings a smile to my face. The Escazu mountains are about one hundred miles away from the property, but they look closer in this light. Especially after last night's rainstorm pushed away all of the clouds that usually try to conceal the mountain's regal peaks. The orange and purple sky is already speckled with stars even though the sun hasn't completely set. I can hear the crickets and creatures in the trees, as I accelerate down the wide gravel pathway onto the concrete driveway. That's when I spotted him. Standing outside of a yellow taxi cab at the delivery entrance of the property with the rear passenger door wide open, wiping the lenses of his glasses with a small cloth that he pulled from his back pocket. He was taller than I expected him to be. About six feet even, wearing khaki slacks, dark brown loafers, a pea soup colored sweater vest, and a disappointed look on his face that I can only assume to be permanent. A pretentious uniform, fitting for someone so ornery.

"Mr. Cardenas?" I asked him with a smile. "In the flesh," he said dryly. "I presume you work for Chef Kababo and he's sent you to collect me?" "Something like that. My name is Brittany, and I'm happy to drive you back to the property." I extended my hand in an attempt to politely shake his before I noticed his critical gaze already beaming over the top of his glasses. He looked at me from my shoes to the top of my head and reluctantly accepted my handshake. "I see," he said. "Well, let the adventure begin." He slammed the car door shut and walked over to the passenger side of the golf cart. I glanced over at the driver who was already shaking his head, which let me know that Cardenas had been everything but an ideal passenger. I sat in the driver's seat and tapped my foot twice on the pedal to disengage the parking brake, and Cardenas immediately reached for the grab handle above his head. "Is everything alright?" "Oh, yes," he said. "Don't mind me, it's just a habit. Can never be too careful." He exhaled deeply then adjusted himself in the seat. I knew right then that tonight's dinner would be unforgettable, and I couldn't wait to get him back to the house.

As we approached the property, I could see one of the staff members out in the garden about 20 feet away, seeding the soil with a spreader. They recognized the cart and waved to me, immediately catching Cardenas' interest. "Does that garden belong to

Chef Kababo?" he asked. "Yep! It's one of the reasons why Chef chose this area for the bed and breakfast. The soil here is very rich, so he's able to produce some really great vegetation". The garden stretches over an acre and a half and includes seemingly endless rows of vegetables and fruit trees. Dark leafy greens emerge from the heaps of soil beneath them reaching toward the skies, alongside fragrant herbs like lemon basil, French thyme, coriander, dill tips and tomato plants.

"That's a major improvement from his days in Houston," he added snarkily. I could tell where the conversation was headed, so I decided to reroute it a bit. "That's right! He's always been an advocate for growing the food that he cooks with and serves to his guests, so now that we have the garden close by, he's able to do so much more than he was able to do back home." Cardenas caught on to my intention, and gave him a sarcastic smile to let him know that I knew the game he was trying to play.

"Is that a greenhouse?" Cardenas asked. I couldn't help but smile, seeing my pride and joy glistening in the moonlight. "Yep! That's my greenhouse", I said. "I've had a thing for plants and flowers for years, so I wanted to have a place for them to thrive that was all their own." Cardenas let out a grunt, indicating that he may have been slightly impressed.

The greenhouse is nestled on the far side of the garden about fifteen feet away from where the sweet potatoes grow, and it was the only request that I had when Chef was developing the blueprints for the property, aside from an obnoxiously large soaking tub for the master bedroom. It's a sixteen by eight foot wonderland surrounded by ivy

and peppercorn trees. It was built with dark plum mahogany beams, double-layered

fiberglass panes and a vaulted twelve foot ceiling with deep purple window panes

throughout. The inside has off-white wood paneling where Chef and I hung a total of 13

shelves to hold my beloved houseplants, along with a wooden platform that serves as a

countertop and propagation station. It's the most dreamy hideaway, and my favorite

place to escape and read a book while sitting in the small white hammock that's

anchored to one of the beams in the ceiling.

"Do you enjoy gardening at all?" I asked him in an effort to spark conversation

again. "Nah. No time really. I'm away from home more often than I'm there, so any

houseplants that I have would definitely die from lack of attention" he said without

looking my way.

We pulled up to the front of the house, and I forgot for a moment how beautiful it

looks from the outside at night. I'm usually inside or in the backyard around this time, so

I made a mental note to venture through the front door more often. The orange and pink

ginger plants stand tall in the front yard next to the anthuriums, adding liveliness to the

overflow of green in the flower beds. "Here we are," I said to him and I returned the golf

cart to its place on the side of the house and invited him to follow me to the party. We

walked into the backyard to see a waiter standing at the entryway into the kitchen with a

tray of delicately decorated crystal tea cups. Each filled with a warm, plum red liquid that

he calls "Chef's Tea" to help warm us up as we come in from the cool night air.

"Chef's Tea?" the waiter says. Halfway asking and half politely suggesting that we take one. I've had this tea many times before and I still don't know what's in it. All I know is that he has some of the herbs flown in from different parts of the world, and some he grows himself. He dries them out or roasts them before steeping them in near boiling water, before passing the mixture through a fine mesh sieve. It's a delicate balance of herbaceous and sweet, fruity and strong, medicinal and intoxicating. And no one can put their finger on exactly what's in it. Everyone takes a tea cup and slowly sips, as they try to figure out the recipe. Some assume there are dried roses or raspberry leaves, and others are simply fascinated by the rich color.

"None for me, thank you.", Cardenas said in a cynical tone. The guests all turned around to see Mr. Cardenas standing there with the same unimpressed expression that he so easily translated to his reviews. "I'd prefer to preserve my palette rather than disturb it. At least until we have dinner. And from my understanding, Chef Kababo is a chef, not a bartender."

I looked over at Dani, who had been overseeing the serving staff at the appetizer spread. Her eyes were wide in disbelief after witnessing Cardenas in all of his obstinate glory. Most of the guests stood in silence with intrigued looks on their faces after hearing his words, but not Lucas. He was already privy to all things Cardenas, thanks to his weekly conversations with Chef.

"Aye, Chef! I have two questions for you" he said, trying to break up the awkward tension. "What's in this tea? I see you sipping on it all the time in the kitchen, but I've never seen you make it!".

Chef smiled. He knew exactly what Lucas was doing, and he appreciated him for it. Miguel raised his glass to interject. "Yeah that tea is good and everything, but I'm going to need the recipe for the Filet Mignon Egg Rolls!", he said with his mouth half full. The rest of us laughed but we were all thinking the same thing.

"Oh you like those huh?" Chef said to Miguel. "What's your second question, Luc?" Chef asked. "Can we get a tour of the house?" he asked with his hands raised in hope.

"Follow me," Chef said.

Filet Mignon Egg Rolls

**Reading the recipe* In the top section you will find everything you will need for this dish so you can gather all of your mise en place (Tools & Things) at one time. Below this section you will find the recipe is broken up into sections using portions of the mise en place.*

Ingredients

All Purpose Flour - 4 c

Cornstarch - for dusting

Salt - 1 tbsp

Water - 1 c

Egg - 1

Beef Tenderloin - 1#

Red Onions - 1 each

Italian Seasoning - 1 tbsp

Smoked Gouda Cheese - ½ #

Dijon Mustard - 2 tbsp

Red Wine Vinegar - 2 c

Horseradish - 1 tbsp

Whole Grain Mustard - 1 tbsp

Sourcream - 1 tbsp

Lime - ½ each

Canola Oil -2L

Tools

Cheese Grater
Rolling Pin
Medium Mixing Bowl
Half Sheet Pan x2
Medium Fry Pot (I use a cast iron pan)
Medium Tongs
Napkins
Wooden Cooking Spoon (optional)

Wonton Wrapper

All Purpose Flour - 4 c
Cornstarch - for dusting
Salt - 1 tbsp
Water - 1 c
Egg - 1

Making this dough is pretty simple, if you have a mixer with a dough hook feel free to use that, however your hands will work just fine. Grab a medium size mixing bowl and add your dry ingredients first, then add the egg & 4c of water to bring it all together.

Stir with a wooden spoon or your hand, the point is to combine everything together so you can knead it for a bit, building up the strength within the dough. Starting the dough in a mixing bowl helps you from spilling water all over your countertop. Once the dough has come together, dust your countertop with cornstarch and begin to knead your dough. You are searching for a consistent smooth surface that is moist but not sticky and elastic. You might have to adjust the amount of water if your dough is too dry or the amount of flour if too wet. I've noticed if the humidity is high, the amount of water changes a bit so just be prepared to make small adjustments depending on the first *outcome. If the dough is too moist add a bit more flour, if the dough is too dry simply add a bit more water. If you are using a mixer, allow the dough to mix for 2-3 mins so you can form some gluten within the dough. This will decrease the chances of the thin wrapper tearing when you are stuffing it with your filling. If you are using your hands, you will want to knead this dough for 5-7 mins to ensure it's strong enough. If you are doing this by hand and at the end of the 5-7 mins the dough isn't smooth, soft, & bouncy keep kneading.*

Once the dough is ready to go, allow it to rest for 15 mins or so before rolling out the wonton sheets. If you have a pasta roller, by all means use that to achieve the traditionally thin pasty wrapper. By using the pasta roller, work your way down to the lowest or second to lowest setting depending on your machine. Be sure to put loose cornstarch onto the machine to prevent the dough from sticking. If you don't have a pasta roller, fear not! Working the dough by hand is fun, and keeps you connected with the experience.

By using a rolling pin and dusting it with cornstarch to prevent the dough from sticking you can accomplish the same result of the pasta roller, it will just take you a bit longer. It should be as thin as 2 or 3 sheets of paper with a height and width of 6 inches x 6 inches. The dough will come out much larger than this and you will have to cut the smaller sheets out of the larger one. Reuse the scraps to make a new ball of dough to roll out once you have accumulated enough dough.

Egg Roll Filling

Beef Tenderloin - 1#

Red Onions - 113g

Italian Seasoning - 1 tbsp

Smoked Gouda Cheese - ½ #

Dijon Mustard - 2 tbsp

Red Wine Vinegar - 2 c

Salt - 1 tbsp

Black Pepper - 1 tbsp

Starting with the tenderloin, dice into ¼ inch pieces, we are going to marinade it in dijon mustard for 1 night (preferred), however you can start the marinade process in the morning and cook it in the evening if you are not prepared to do the whole overnight thing. Flavor is everything to my culture and the marinade process is just another way to add another layer of flavor into the dish. You are only using enough mustard to lightly cover the tenderloin so don't go overboard because the dish will be off balance with a strong dijon mustard flavor.

Sauce

Horseradish - 1 tbsp grated

Whole Grain Mustard - 1 tbsp

Sourcream - 1 tbsp

Lime - ½ each

In a mixing bowl place all of the ingredients and mix together.

As far as the pickled red onions, you'll want to start these at the same time you begin marinating the tenderloin. Fine Julienne slice the red onion & combine the red wine vinegar and Italian seasoning into a bowl large enough to completely cover the red onion. Allow to sit for 1 day (prefered) or you can start this process in the morning and have it ready to cook that same evening.

Using a cheese grater, finely shred the smoked gouda cheese.
Mix all of the ingredients (beef, pickled red onions, & smoked gouda cheese) together in a mixing bowl and season the food with a bit of salt & pepper (2 pinches or so).

To make this a bit easier we are going to label each corner of the square wonton wrapper (1,2,3,4). Corners 1 & 3 should point to your left and right respectively. You are going to place the filling diagonally across the wonton wrapper (1 to 3), leaving about an inch on each side. Now take corners (1 & 3) and fold them on top of the filling, they should be pointing towards one another, they were once pointed in opposite directions before you just folded them. With corner 2 pointing towards you, fold on top the filling across corners 1 & 3 towards corner 4 and pull the filling towards you a bit to have a snug fit within the wonton wrapper. Once the filing is snug and tight you will begin to roll corner 2 towards corner 4 to complete the eggroll. Take a little splash of water and douse corner 4 so that it will stick and hold in place once the roll is completed. The eggroll should be without rips and firmly in place. Sprinkle some flour all over the egg roll and place onto a sheet pan while you continue to prepare the remaining egg rolls. It's best to douche the entire egg roll with a light coat of flour to prevent sticking.

With canola oil at 325 degrees you will fry your egg rolls until golden brown (about 3-5 mins). Place onto a napkin so they can cool a bit after frying to remove the extra oil.. Don't go on time, look for the golden brown color and once you see that it's done. Once cooled, cut the egg rolls in half diagonally and cross them on top of each other onto the plate.

You can place this sauce in a small ramekin to dip your egg roll in or you can be fancy and make a swoosh across the plate making it artsy!
–Kababo

Chapter 4

Tea for the Ego

Genius & the Fool, as a sophomore in high school I decided to grow an afro and braid my hair to the great disappointment of my grandparents. It was honestly just a phase that I would have quickly passed through, however my lovely grandmother pressed the issue, challenging me on how I will never make it in this world with my hair like that. So 10 years later, after I've done fairly well for myself as a braided up black man in the American south, I cut my hair off.
– Kababo

One by one, Paola, Miguel, Kamryn, Lucas, Dani, Mr. Cardenas and I followed Chef as he stepped down into the spacious open concept family room. We were welcomed by neutral colored plush sectional seating, large enough to comfortably accommodate Chef's tall frame and several other people. The room has a warm and inviting feel, and is the kind of living room that you'd want to spend Friday nights playing games in with your loved ones. A wide wall of windows let in the moonlight, making it the best place to view the backyard and all of the Costa Rican jungle behind it.

In the center of the room is a one of a kind limestone coffee table. We found it last year at a quirky local furniture store that was having a going out of business sale. The whole store smelled like cedar chests and rain, and we almost didn't see the table because it was hidden beneath stacks of books with worn and tattered pages. The salesman was a sweet older man, small in stature, who wore a brown plaid shirt and green suspenders. When we asked where the table was from, he let a sly smile crawl across his face as he told us that it was either given to him in a will from a very rich family member that had passed away or he found it on the side of the road, but that if we could haul the table out of the store ourselves he would give it to us for fifty dollars. That was all it took for Chef to laugh and hand over the money. Now, the coffee table is home to a couple of magazines with his face on the cover.

Chef took a seat on one of the arms of the couch and stretched his long legs out in front of him with his hands in his pockets, as he surveyed the room from the perspective of his guests. Miguel and Paola noticed the framed photos on top of the black rectangular shelving unit that held rows of vinyl records and books behind the couch. "Look at you! You were so young!", Paola said. Chef smiled a half smile at the photo of his eight year old self, wearing Wrangler jeans, dark brown cowboy boots and a red button up shirt and holding hands with his parents. "Yeah, I had to have been in the second grade there. It was Western Day at school, and all the kids had to dress up in their western gear like cowboys," Chef said as he held the frame.

"That must be a Texas thing, huh?" Miguel asked jokingly. "Definitely a Texas thing, but we thought it was normal. Now that I think about it, there are a lot of things that we grew up with that we thought were normal that actually turned out to only be native to Texas", he said laughing at the thought.

"Wow Chef..Your mother is beautiful in this photo," Dani said. "How is she holding up in Houston with you being so far away?" At that moment, those of us that knew the story of Kababo's beloved mother had a swell in our hearts. "Unfortunately, she passed away from cancer in 2019." He said with a sad smile on his face. "I was able to be by her side when she transitioned though, so that's something that I'll hold close to my heart forever." We could all tell that Dani immediately felt awful for having asked the question in the first place, but Chef put his hand on top of her head in the big brother way that he always does, letting her know that everything was okay. "You know, I don't see death as a sad punctuation to a life lived," he said. "I see it as a graduation, something to be celebrated when achieved. So while I miss her every day, and would love to have her here with me tangibly, I know that she's with me spiritually, and I honor her in everything that I do," he said. "Do you mind sharing what she was like?" Dani asked, hoping that the question would spark pleasant memories and dissolve any awkwardness she may have caused. He exhaled deeply as he stroked at his long neatly braided beard tucked under his chin. "Aw man," he started. "I know a lot of people say that they have the best mom in the world, but my mom was truly one of one. She was the most amazing woman, with a heart bigger than anyone I've ever met. We always had a lot of fun together, but her favorite thing to do was make the two hour drive to the casino with her sisters and play Roulette and Blackjack."

His parents had Kababo when they were really young; his mom was 19 and his dad only 16 at the time. The three of them grew up together, and despite them moving around a lot to different apartments in the Greenspoint area of Houston, his mom always made sure that the whole extended family spent a lot of time together. Family means the world to him, and he makes sure to keep in touch with everyone back home as much as he can.

Just as we were looking through the rest of Chef's childhood photos, we heard a knock at the front door. I jogged over to open it and saw Tory standing there with his signature ear-to-ear grin, and a duffle bag on his shoulder.

"Hey, B!" he said as he wrapped his long arms around my shoulders to hug me. It had been awhile since we last saw each other, so the hug was long overdue. "Look at you! How was your flight?" I asked. "Did he tell you I missed my first flight?" he said as he winced a bit. He knows his big brother well enough to know that no matter what he does or how many kid brother mistakes he makes, Chef will always have his back. "I got on another flight like an hour after that though, so it was cool! I forgot how dope it was to fly over water like that." He walked inside and carelessly dropped his bag down at the entryway, immediately distracted by the details of the house that we added since the last time he visited. "Is everyone here already?" he asked. "Yeah, and you'll never guess who else showed up." He raised an eyebrow at me, the same way his brother does. "Come on, he's about to give a tour for everybody". We walked over to the rest of the group in the family room and Chef immediately lit up at the sight of his brother. "Speaking of family," Chef said, "this is my baby brother, Tory! Late to the party as usual, but we're happy to have him!" The two exchanged a quick hug before Tory found Kamryn in the crowd and went over to nag at her like he always does.

Chef picked up another picture frame and told us he doesn't have many photos from his childhood due to an accidental closet fire that destroyed most of them. "This one was taken when we lived in an apartment in Northchase. I remember I had a crush on a girl named Jessica who lived in our apartment complex!" By now, a bigger smile

begins to show on his face. I thought she was beautiful, and all I wanted to do was save

up enough money to buy her a dress so that I could take her out on a date." Everyone

laughed at the thought of the man we see in front of us being so small, and yet so

determined.

"I wanted to take her out on that date so badly, so in my mind, the only logical

thing to do was to start a business that would make me some money. My mom told me

that I ran home and couldn't wait to tell her all about this frozen Cool Cups business

idea. In the hood, there was always a Candy Lady. A sweet older woman who was kind

of like an auntie to everyone on the block. She would stock up on candy at wholesale

stores, so the kids in the neighborhood could come to her house and buy candy from

her. I saw that there was a Candy Lady house, but recognized that there was a market

for Cool Cups! So I executed. My mom helped me to get all the supplies, and I did the

math to figure out what price point would bring in the best profit. Twenty five cents for

regular Cool Cups and fifty cents for the ones with big gumballs in the bottom. What's

most ironic to me about this story is that this is right around the time that my elementary

school teacher suggested that I be moved from regular education to Special Education

classes. It was clear that I didn't have a mental or learning deficit, and of course my

mother knew that as well. But after watching me develop a business plan and bring it to

life at such a young age solidified that I was not only intelligent, but determined. My

entire family is made up of business owners, so when it comes to thinking about how to

make money, my first thought is to start a business. Working for someone else never crossed my mind, only how to get my own money because that's what I saw my family do. My mom thought it was so funny that her eight year old kid came up with the idea to start a business and actually carried it out. All because I wanted to take a little girl out on a date!"

"So you were good with the ladies and a businessman back then, huh?" asked Miguel. "I did the best I could with the ladies, man!", Chef jokingly replied. "I come from a long line of hard workers though. My mom worked retail for most of my life, and my dad worked as a cook at restaurants and hotels for a while. My grandmother was an entrepreneur, and my aunts and uncles worked hard in their fields as well. We all worked hard, but nothing was more important than spending time together. My family is extremely tight-knit, and we always have each other's back. I spent a lot of time with my grandmother on my mom's side because she lived in the same apartment complex as us. So after school I would go to her house and hang out until my mom or dad came home."

"We were really close. My mom always believed in my ideas, and never once told me that I couldn't do something. That's probably why I'm so fearless now. Even though I was a mama's boy, I was also really independent and she really understood my need for freedom and creativity. I definitely appreciated that."

"Have you been able to spend time with the family since you've moved out here?", Mr. Cardenas asked. "Obviously not as much as I would like to, but we talk often. They played a huge part in my move here, and always encouraged me to pursue whatever dreams or goals that I had. My family is what drives me. They're the reason why I work so hard. I love the artistry of culinary, and I'm passionate about what I do. But I do it all for my family. I want to leave a legacy of smart work, and for the fruits of my labor to benefit my bloodline."

Chef led us from the family room into the massive foyer, and the guests were immediately taken aback at the boldness of the space. Deep purple drapes cascade from the ceiling to the floor of the foyer entrance, framing the massive double front doors, and sweeping the polished blue marble floors. On the left side of the foyer sits a sparkling gold pond surrounded by smooth river rocks and bright green foliage. A few guests step over to it and watch for a moment as the four shimmering orange and white koi fish chase each other in the depths of the water. The pond is serene and brings a fresh palate cleansing to the inescapable extravagance of the room.

Dramatic, moody lighting set the tone for the entire house, but the foyer is full of undeniable grandeur. High ceilings serve as a canvas to the focal point of the room. The most elaborate cascading crystal chandelier with what looks like a million long diamond drop earrings repelling from the top of the fixture. It's undeniable size is reminiscent of the kind of chandeliers that you would expect to find at a fancy New York City hotel, or maybe ~~even~~ living among royalty. You have to walk around the perimeter of the room in order to fully experience all of its details. It's almost too big for the room, taking up nearly all of the air and space in the same way that his insecurities and ego used to do years ago. Demanding attention and giving the observer the impression that it's braggadocio was there to cover up some massive insecurity or blemish.

I remember Chef telling me that he wanted the foyer to be symbolic of his character when he was younger. A larger than life personality, with even bigger insecurities. "That's what the ego does", he said. "It can't see itself because it's so fucking big, but it serves it's purpose of hiding all of the insecurities. Ego lies, blocks, fills up the empty spaces and scratches to protect the owner from those weaknesses for survival purposes." And it does. The foyer is elaborate and eye-catching, but also an optical illusion. It seemingly changes depth and width depending on where the viewer stands in the room. In the same way that someone can only see into the exposed and vulnerable parts of another person. The look and feel of it changes and morphs with perspective.

Things came easily to him. He never really had to work too hard at mastering things, because he's truly good at just about everything; which has proven to not always be a good thing. "When you're used to being good at everything, failure can be soul-crushing," he said. " You begin to question yourself and your abilities, and for me, I obsessed over whatever that thing was to the point where I would not stop thinking about it until I either mastered it, or understood how I could master it. Once I got to that point, I could let it go and leave it alone and move on to the next thing."

That's one of the many things about him that has always fascinated me. Partly because my brain doesn't function that way, and I let things be difficult and accept that maybe some things just aren't for me. But not him. He never thinks that way. He looks at life from a completely different perspective, and he moves through it all with an audacity that many don't understand. He has this unbridled confidence that assures him that there is absolutely nothing that he cannot master, accomplish, or become great at. Fear doesn't exist in his world, and it's almost unfathomable to him that other people allow themselves to be ruled by it.

All of that confidence and fearlessness has contributed to his arrogance, which lets him border on the edge of narcissism at times. The cards have always been in his favor since before he was born. He's the first born son, the favorite grandchild, and everyone's favorite relative. But that can be incredibly heavy to carry, yet somehow he's managed to carve out his own unconventional path for himself.
"This is probably one of my favorite parts of the house", he says, as the rest of us stood in awe at the high ceiling, trying to soak in every tiny detail that makes up the space.

"The foyer reminds me a lot of my grandmother. She owned an interior decorating company when I was young, and she had a reputation in the rich parts of town for creating some of the most amazing and unique interior designs for her clients. Word spread about her like wildfire, and pretty soon after she got started, all the rich ladies in the neighborhood wanted Shirley Green of Green's Interior Design to come and decorate their homes. She would bring me along with her to help her carry fabrics and pillows, or help her hang things since I was so tall. I watched how she created a

successful business around her God-given talent, and how important it was for her to

have an accountant and CPA on staff to keep the books in line. I've modeled a lot of my

business structure after her." It was true. Everything about his business practices was

emulated after his grandmother. The way he negotiated deals, never accepting the first

offer because no one presents their best rate upfront was all Ms. Shirley Green. The

high ceiling and marble floors make room for the echo of his voice as he shared

memories of his grandmother, and pointed out parts of the room that were designed to

honor her.

"She pretty much raised me", Chef said as he walked up to a beautifully framed

photo of his grandmother that sat in a built-in nook that was likely created just for the

frame. "I was a super creative kid who could never sit still. I always had to be moving, or

playing or creating something. My mom told me years ago when I was a kid, my favorite

toys were the clothes hangers that she would bring home from her job at the

department store. The plastic ones with the little metal clips at the top that would push

up and down to clamp pants or jeans in them. I could sit and play with a hanger for

hours, and never get bored of it. In my mind, it was everything but a hanger. It was the

handlebars to a make believe motorcycle, or a helicopter when I would spin the curved

handle top around my finger so fast it only looked like a blur. It could also be a steering

wheel of a car I would hold onto with both hands and run through the house with."

Chapter 5

Chef Longblade

My first official job outside of my Grandmother's family business was at the age of 16 working for Old Navy in the shipping department. We would begin work at 9p and get off at 1a, then I would wake up and be at high school for 7a. I don't know what's more amazing, the fact that I did that or that my mother supported it. That woman was so special and the fact that she was my mother was just a homerun. She always supported my ambitions even when the ideas were out of this world. About a year later I became a salesman at Sears in the small electronics department and my shift started at 4pm. I would leave varsity basketball practice early so I could be to work on time and the Coach didn't really think I was focused on basketball, and he was right.
– Kababo

Chef took the lead and guided us out of the foyer and into the hallway that led to his office space. An oversized desk made of brushed concrete is angled on one side of the room, next to gray file cabinets and plush leather office chairs. Above his desk hangs a gallery-style collection of his favorite anime characters like Afro Samurai, Goku, and Yasuke along with a signed sketch of Chef Longblade, the main character of a series called Chef Gods. Chef Longblade is an elephant-faced demigod called a "Monkeyphant". He's a chef prodigy, and carries two long ass blades with him at all times, just in case someone wants to battle him in the kitchen. The show debuted in Japan and gained worldwide popularity after the book series was released in the United States. Kamryn and her friends became obsessed with the books and she told her dad all about them, and he was instantly hooked too. Now, the three of us anxiously await new episodes and binge watch them together.

"This is where all the business deals go down!" Chef said proudly. "And these guys help me to stay focused and grounded as I make the moves that I make every day."

Lucas is also an anime fan, so he was fascinated by the art on the walls and did his best to contain his excitement. "Hey Chef," Miguel started. "Back in the foyer, you mentioned your grandmother was an entrepreneur too, right?"

"Yeah, and she was really good at it until she wasn't. She showed me the first checks that I had ever seen and they were all five figures, and in my mind I thought that was a normal amount of money for anyone to make. When I got my first check from my retail gig at Old Navy when I was a teenager and it was only a few hundred dollars, I figured out the only way I could make the kind of money that I wanted was to work for myself. My grandmother would always say 'don't be crumbin! Ask for your money. Go for big money, and don't play small.' A lot of my spirit and ingenuity comes from her, and the other part comes from time I spent working for corporate America."

"That makes a lot of sense. I can't imagine working for a major corporation for years, only to make the CEO rich. And then having no time or energy left to work toward your own goals," Miguel said. Miguel has only ever known entrepreneurship from the lens of his family business, so the thought of making money for anyone other than his family was absurd to him. Chef was the same way, and that's part of the reason why they connected so well as friends. They related to each other when it came to business and believe that the most important goal that anyone can have in their work is to build generational wealth that would ultimately feed their families for generations.

"Right! I didn't work for other people often, but when I did, it drove me crazy. I watched how companies did business and compared it to what I watched my grandmother do. I took it and applied it to my own ventures so that I could better provide for my family, and made sure to eliminate the worst of both. While my grandmother largely had a successful business for most of my childhood, she also couldn't control her spending. She liked nice things, and always had the most beautiful things in her home. Collectively, they were more expensive than the home itself, and it was worth over two million dollars. It was cool to watch her become so successful, but as sad as it was, I also needed to see her lose it. I think watching her spending habits taught me how important it is to not overspend. For some people, overspending is something that they can come back from. But for me, if I were to do that, it would be detrimental to my family dynasty. If I didn't learn from the successes and failures of the people before me, then I would have done a disservice to my bloodline. That goes for you all as well. We have a choice to challenge and change the way things have always been in our families, or to continue the same cycles. I chose to take what was, and transform it into something greater. And I work at it every day."

Dani walked over to the desk and noticed a cold, half empty mug of tea resting on a coaster next to the large curved gaming monitor that's sprawled with multi-colored graphs going every which way to indicate the day's trading progress.

"Chef, you gotta let me come in here and help you clean up," she said to him in jest. "I know right?" he said as he smiled at her offer. "That's just from this morning though. I'm not a messy guy!"

Lucas stood behind the desk chair, his gaze now focused on the day trading graphs on the monitor screen. "Chef, I didn't know you were into stocks like that!" he said. Chef quickly cocked his head to the side in amusement and raised an eyebrow at him. "What did you think I meant when I told you and Dani all those times to invest your money?"

"I don't know," Lucas answered sheepishly. "I thought that was just something that people with money say to people that don't have any," he said with a shrug. Chef had no choice but to laugh. "I try to start every morning the same way. I wake up, stretch a little bit, check on my plants, make a cup of my tea, then come in here to the office to prepare for the stock market and daily trading before I dive into any paperwork of business for the property."

"So wait," Lucas started. He was dumbstruck and it was evident in the confused look on his face. He had been working for Chef for a couple of years now, and thought he knew a lot about him, but was surprised to learn about his interests in finance. "How long have you been doing stocks and all this stuff?" he asked.

"I've been working with stocks and trading since I was about 15 or so. I started out by playing a Stock Market game for kids with my cousin, and we got really into it. My uncle taught us about the highs and lows of trading, and he actually invested a lot of money into AOL shortly before it went bust, so he took that pretty hard. I became fascinated with the market in the fall of 2007, and how it ebbs and flows so differently every day, so I bought a ton of books and learned as much as I could about trading. Like a lot of people, I ended up losing a lot of money when the market crashed in 2008, probably about $30K. It was heartbreaking and extremely painful, and I actually stopped trading for a long time. It wasn't until 2020 that I got really good at stocks and trading, even though there have been more losses than wins." Chef would talk about finances and the stock market for hours if he was given the opportunity. He loves food and all things culinary, but he might love the energy that comes with making money even more.

"So what advice would you give to someone who wants to learn about stocks and trading?" Paola asked him. Miguel was shocked by her sudden interest in the conversation topic, but he didn't let her know it.
Chef loves it when people ask him this question because he can tell that whoever is asking is genuinely interested in learning what he has to share. "I would tell them to read and study about it as much as they can," he told her. "They should understand that there are several ways to go about trading. For me, it was a lengthy and expensive process but it's taught me a lot about how to manage money better, and how I can build wealth."

"I feel like the whole concept of the stock market is confusing, and it doesn't make sense to me that we all weren't exposed to it when we were growing up," Tory said. He and Chef have conversations about investing and finance all the time, but I think Tory is more interested in accumulating as much money as he can right now. Which isn't far off from what his brother's motive was when he was in his twenties himself.

"A lot of people in our community are not afforded the opportunity to learn about or be exposed to stocks. There's definitely an entrance barrier, and a lot of the information that's out there is made to sound more complicated than it is," Chef said with his hand stroking his long beard. "I remember one time back in 2007, I was on the phone with a customer service guy from TradeKing, a trading platform from back in the day that would charge $5 per trade. The trade fee was a barrier to keep regular people from trading, and now there are a ton of platforms that allow you to trade for free. The guy was so surprised that I was black and knew so much about trading, and said that he wished more people in our community had access to trading. The cost of entry to get into the stock market already excluded poor people, but the entire system wasn't designed for middle or lower class folks." At this point in the conversation, Miguel, Tory and Lucas are completely engaged.

"Now that retail investors are allowed to have a piece of the pie, it's sort of like what happened with prohibition, right? Pretty much anyone can do it now," Miguel added.

"Exactly," Chef said with a snap of his fingers for emphasis. "I look at the stock market and trading as a tool, and if used correctly it can serve as another stream of income. There's a pool of unlimited money and it's connected to a complex equation. But if you can figure it out, you can tap into it and it will free you from worrying about how you are going to pay for things. Once I realized that, I couldn't let it go. I was compelled to figure it out. Learning the stock market is like learning humans. When you learn that, you will win. We do the same things over and over again. We are creatures of habit. You can make money off of that if you pay attention to the trends."

"So how did covid and the pandemic affect your businesses back in 2020?" Miguel asked.

"Oh man, it definitely took a major hit. Before covid, I was doing a lot of private cooking for clients, and catering for parties and events almost every month. But covid pretty much demolished the catering industry during that time," Chef started. "Thankfully, I was able to secure the SBA loan from the government but the loan was only helpful to those who had been helping themselves up to that point. I have a small business, but I make sure that my paperwork and taxes are all in line the same way that a major corporation would have. I have no doubt that we wouldn't have survived without that loan. I've always been very meticulous when it comes to business and paperwork, and I credit that to my grandmother too," he said.

This is exactly why Chef started CPC Academy. He wanted to teach others about stocks and trading and how it can benefit them. Some might wonder what those things have to do with culinary, but it's absolutely related. When he wasn't able to be in the kitchen for his private clients or catering events, Chef was still able to make money without stressing about how to make ends meet.

"I was still bringing in revenue when one part of my business was out of commission," he said. "My career plan was never about just cooking and being in the kitchen. I wanted it to be multifaceted, but to still have some connection to the culinary world. And I encourage everyone to do the same. Find your gifts, your talents and your natural interests. Whatever you're good at. Take out a piece of paper, and write down ten things that are connected to that talent and how you can monetize it, then, execute. When you do it that way, you set yourself up to have your gifts make room for you. That one talent can be used to make money for you directly and passively if you want it to. In my opinion, that's the best way to make the most of your talents and fully enjoy life at the same time," he said.

Cardenas had been quiet for most of the tour, but at this point in the conversation his interest was piqued, likely because he had only known Kababo as a Chef. The thought of him being anything other than that, or having any other interests was surprising. "So, I have to ask you," Cardenas started. "How are you able to explore all of these side interests while maintaining a thriving culinary career?" His tone was judgemental, flat and condescending, exactly like his writing.

"Well to be honest, if I were still an Executive Chef, there's no way that I would be able to pick up and start a new business in another country! I would be in the kitchen all day, every day, non stop. You remember what that's like, don't you Mr. Cardenas?" With a smug look on his face, Cardenas nodded his head in acknowledgement of Chef's statement. "Working that many hours is hard on your body, and especially hard on your mental and emotional health," Chef added. "A lot of people see the title of Executive Chef, and automatically think about the celebrity status that comes with it. Which, I personally don't understand why that's a thing, but that's neither here nor there. What they don't see are the hours of preparation, planning, menu prep, staff issues, leadership problems, vendor issues, management, and customer issues. Not to mention the strain that all of that can put on your personal life. There's none of that. An Executive Chef is lucky to have any personal life outside of the kitchen, because all of their time, energy and effort has to be focused on the kitchen."

"So is that all you do here? Make deals and run the business?" Tory asked his brother sarcastically. Chef let out a big loud laugh. "No big deal right? I also do a little bit of gaming here and there, but not at all like I used to."
Video games were his first love. He grew up playing everything from Atari to Nintendo to Doom on PC and Wolfenstein 3D.
"You like to game too? Since when?" Lucas asked him in shock. "Man what? I'm an old school gamer and have been playing since I was a kid. I loved all those old school first person shooter games, and I would play all the time with my Uncle and his friends and we'd have LAN parties!" Chef replied.

Chef was clearly showing his age with his gaming references and Tory and Lucas caught on to it as they exchanged glances. "LAN parties? That's old school for real," Tory said with a laugh.

"Most definitely! We would all go over to my uncle's house with our game consoles and play for hours. That was way before wifi and streaming and the ability to make crazy money off of gaming. Now, you can make a really good living off of gaming full time, which was completely unheard of when I was coming up. Being a gaming streamer would have been my dream job when I was younger for sure."

"What do you like to play now?" Lucas asked him. "My all-time favorite PC games are League of Legends. Hands down," Chef said to him.
Excitement erupted from Tory and Lucas, as the game is a favorite among their friends. "I used to play League of Legends for hours, but had to stop because of the stress it was causing me. I love competitive games, but cooking and being stressed out about business made me anxious and it manifested in some pretty intense physical pain. Every time I played League of Legends, the high APM or actions per minute would be so stressful for me that it would aggravate my stomach, but I couldn't stop playing! The high intensity of the competition was addicting, but I had to let it go for the sake of my career. I vowed to stop playing because I wouldn't have been able to become a successful chef. I didn't play video games again for years outside of little games on my cell phone like Chess or Boom Beach. They were temporary fixes to hold me over until I

was able to get back to real gaming. I had every intention of going back to League of

Legends, but now it's really dependent on my health."

Dani and I exchanged glances and I knew she was going to ask the obvious

question. "Chef, I don't think I understand. If the game is so stressful to watch and play,

what do you like about it and why do you keep going back to it?" she asked him.

Chef looked right at me and I just shook my head, knowing full well what his

answer was going to be. "It's fun because it's competitive and you can kick someone's

ass!" he said with enthusiasm. "That's what keeps me going back every few years. I

love it."

Chapter 6

The Spine

My favorite musical artists are Prince, Eryka Bydu, Nas, Hans Zimmer, and Scarface. My favorite books are The Black Sun by Peter Moon, Isis Unveiled by H.P Blavatsky, Ancient Egypt: The Light Of The World by Gerald Massey, and The Sirius Mystery by Robert Temple. Favorite movies are The Matrix, Predator 2, Glass, and Flight. Favorite Anime series because I'm a huge anime head, Dragon Ball Z, Baki, FullMetal Alchemist, Seven Deadly Sins, and Fate. And last but not least my favorite video games are The Stock Market, League Of Legends, Starcraft 1, Doom 2, Half Life 1, Street Fighter 2, Mortal Kombat 2, Diablo 2, & Tekken 3 and yes the stock market is most definitely a video game. Clicking the mouse on my computer just like all the other pc games out there.

-Kababo

We filed out of the office and walked toward the hallway, which is the main artery of the house. Cool marble floors beneath us carry our voices and the sound of our footsteps down the long corridor. To our left stand the built-in waist high cabinets that stretch the entire length of the corridor, topped with several framed photos of some very important people in Chef's life, along with various knick knacks and relics that come with significant stories of their own. Lucas spotted a photo of a much younger version of Chef, sporting traditional chef whites and his signature smile from his time working at a country club.

"When was this photo, Chef?" he asked, smiling down at the photograph. "Wow. This was right at the beginning of my professional career. Look at the look on my face," Chef said. He was immediately taken back to those long nights and even longer days after he had graduated culinary school. He was so determined to take what he had learned and turn it into something bigger than himself. "I was hungry and driven. My whole mentality was about hustling hard, and working on little to no sleep so that I could get closer to that fake finish line. You know that idealized dream that we are all told to have. The one that we're told will make us a happier and wealthier version of ourselves. It's like as soon as we somehow get closer to it, the finish line moves further and further away. Like a dangling carrot on a string that keeps us on a hamster wheel, with the promise of attaining something that we otherwise wouldn't have."

"That whole mindset is laid out for us when we're kids, and we're expected to follow through with it because that's what the American Dream is all about," I added. "Hustle hard. Give your all to your desk job or whatever profession you choose, and work that same job until you're too old to work it anymore. Then take whatever money you've managed to save up, and do your best to enjoy it before you die."

"Yes!" Dani said. She knew about the topic all too well. The first born daughter of hardworking parents and three siblings to look after. "I watched my parents and grandparents give themselves completely to the same job day after day for years, and they felt a sense of pride in having done it because society tells them that working hard until you die is the only way to have a life worth living." Lucas glared at her. "Yeah, but they were hustlers! They taught us the value of working hard for your family, and what it means to be a supportive family."

"At what cost though, Luc? They didn't realize that all of that work took a toll on us. Our parents were there every day, but they were exhausted and unhappy. They were distant, and we grew up thinking that that was the way adulthood and making a living was supposed to be. They projected that idealized mindset of what they were told success had to look like onto us, and they expected us to do the same thing. Don't you remember how miserable it made them?"

Lucas paused for a beat as he thought about his childhood, and how most of his memories were with Dani and his siblings, and their grandmother, and his parents were usually working or resting from their day jobs. "I guess you're right. I didn't think about it like that. I just remember hearing them talk all the time about the importance of working hard, but you're right. They were always working or distant when they were home."

Dani could see that her brother's perspective was much different from hers because she was there to bear the brunt of the pressure, and in that moment she chose to have grace for him. "Exactly, they were always tired and always striving," she said. "I want us to choose to pursue better. A life with balance."

"That's exactly what it's all about. Balance. That's good that you both recognize the cycle that your parents and grandparents were in," Chef said to them. "The best part about it all is that we can choose our reality, and design the life that we want to live. So do that."

Lucas leaned into his sister and she playfully put her arm around his neck. "How did you get off of that hamster wheel of constantly working, Chef?" Lucas asked him. With a deep breath, Chef laid the picture frame back in its place and leaned against the cabinet.

"Man, my body is what forced me to stop. On Christmas Eve of 2017, I was preparing a dinner party for twelve guests for my favorite clients, The Faribais. Normally, I would've had a team to help me prepare and serve, but because of the holiday I couldn't find anyone that was available so I decided to do it on my own."

"Wait a minute," Paola stopped him and reached out her hand as if to stop him in his tracks. "You cooked for twelve people, and did the set up and preparation and everything all by yourself?". She was stunned and maybe even a little disappointed in him at this point.

"I did. But cooking for twelve people isn't out of the norm for me," he assured her. "I noticed that I was running behind, so I was in a rush when I started to load a cooler up onto the back of my truck before heading to their house, and immediately felt extreme tightness and pain shooting down my down and down my left leg. At that moment, I knew I had a decision to make - I could either call off the party because of the injury and intense pain I was in, or push through and keep my commitment to my favorite clients." "I already know you pushed through it, didn't you Chef?" Lucas said with a proud smile on his face.

"Yep! Because I'm a little off my rocker, I pushed through it. I think I found some Ibuprofen or something in my truck and took a couple of those, and drove to their home in the most pain I've ever felt. I had to go in and out of the house to unload the truck, so I would take short breaks in between that time to go and lay on the bathroom floor on my back. I remember the cold marble floor felt amazing on my back, so I did that about three or four times just to get some relief. Finally I couldn't take it anymore when I was damn near about to pass out from the pain, and I went and laid down on the living room floor on my back."

"What were the clients saying to you?" Miguel asked. "Did they notice you were in pain?"

"They did. Mrs. Faribai came into the living room and asked what was wrong, and I told her what happened and that I felt like I was about to die. She walked to her bathroom and returned with a gallon sized plastic bag that was filled with medication bottles. She rummaged through the bottles and when she found one she wanted, she handed me a small pill. I was reluctant to take it because, as you all know, I don't take medication very often. But I was in so much pain that I took it, and I swear that to this day I don't know what that pill was but it was like magic and it helped me get through the rest of the night. I was able to finish the food and serve everyone, and even ended up eating with them and enjoying conversation at the table for a few hours. Everything was great! I packed up at the end of the night and went home."

"What happened after that? Were you just fine?" Dani asked. "Oh, shortly after that I was diagnosed with a 7x13mm fragment on my fifth lumbar, and had to have surgery in June of 2018 to remove the fragment."

Paola and Miguel winced at the thought of the pain Chef must have felt due to the injury and the surgery.

"Please learn from my mistakes and experiences, and prioritize your own health and wellbeing ahead of your work and career. It's never worth it to burn yourself out to the point of severe pain or exhaustion for the sake of your job" he said. "I had to go through a brutal battle with Workers' Compensation to even get the care that I needed at the time. I did everything from physical therapy to occupational therapy and deep tissue massages, but nothing relieved the pain. I finally went in to see a surgeon and was able to schedule spinal surgery. But even that was a struggle." "What do you mean?" Lucas asked. "It was a whole thing. The surgeon suggested steroid injections initially and told me that if his brother were in the same kind of pain that I was in, he would suggest that he have the injections. Maybe I read too much into it, but I went home and looked up the doctor on the internet and found that he didn't have any siblings at all."

"Yikes.. That's pretty intense." "It definitely was for sure. And maybe he was trying to comfort me, or provide me with some sort of encouragement to get the injections. But either way, it taught me a lot about who I am as a person."
Delicately placed picture frames holding the memories of some of the people that helped Chef get to where he is today. Teachers, mentors, friends, and family that all enriched his life in some way.

Chapter 7

Crown Chakra (sahasrara)

Leaving the long hallway behind us, we turned to the left to see double doors standing ten feet high. Chef placed his long hands on each of the knobs, opening the doors wide to the master bedroom. He likes to call it "an oasis hidden inside paradise", and it's his favorite part of the house. Two walls of windows intersect at the southeast corner of the room, giving an incredible view of the jungle surrounding the house, and adding a vastness to the room. A California King sized bed nestled against a stained wood headboard is pushed against the west wall facing the east window, while small potted plants rest on top so that they can stretch wide and soak in the morning sun. Above the bed is a breathtaking ten-foot wide skylight, carved out of the ceiling to look like a telescope into the heavens. On clear nights, it's the perfect place to stare at the sky in awe, and on overcast rainy days it's the best place to take a nap.

Adjacent to the bed are two brown leather chaise lounges and a round wooden coffee table between them. A rolling tray and a black lighter lay next to a deck of oracle cards on the table, with The Emperor card showing upright on top of the deck from the last time he pulled from the deck. This is where he likes to sit and talk on the phone to loved ones, or reflect on the day with a blunt and bourbon. No television or computers for entertainment, only a record player that belonged to his father in the 70's, crates of records, and a bookcase filled with new and old copies of things he's read. The faint scent of recently burned tobacco and patchouli incense hung in the air, adding warmth to the room. This is his sanctuary. His church. Where he comes to collect himself, surrender, be free, and rest. There were comments from the group about the beauty of the room, and they weren't exaggerating at all. The room is stunning, and exactly the kind of bedroom that one could only hope to have.

"This is where I look forward to coming to every day, " Chef shared. "Aside from the kitchen, It's easily my favorite part of the house. I feel like your bedroom should be your sanctuary, and it should only be shared or seen by those that you love and trust. Which is why I've invited you all to see it."

Tory, Lucas and Miguel walked over to the sitting area to try out the chairs and enjoy the view, while Paola and Dani were drawn to the built-in bookcase that nearly spanned the entire length of the wall. It held Chef's eclectic collection of books on various topics like agriculture, Ancient Egyptian Pharaohs, philosophy, history, occult, spirituality and religion. I always say that you can tell a lot about a person based on the books in their home. For example, if someone has a lot of poetry by Pablo Neruda and Maya Angelou, it's probably safe to say that they have an appreciation for life and beautiful lessons that can come in all forms. Kababo's collection only solidifies the fact that he cannot be pegged as anything other than a unique individual with an array of interests.

"What have you been reading about lately?" Paola asked him.
"I like to learn about a few things at once, so right now I'm reading about the diet of Ancient Egyptians and the history of farming in Africa."

Dani pulled a book by Oswald Chambers from the shelf, a famous Christian evangelical teacher from the twentieth century, and gently traced her fingers across the cover. "Do you consider yourself to be a religious person?" she asked him. "I wouldn't," Chef replied after pausing for a few seconds to think about his response. "I'm definitely a spiritual person, but I don't consider myself to be religious. I used to be dedicated to Christianity, and I credit that time in my life to guiding me to pursue a career in culinary. It was during a rough time in my life, and I had been listening to nothing but T.D. Jakes sermons and worship songs to soothe and encourage myself. I remember asking God for a sign about the next steps that I should take, and as soon as the words left my mouth, I got a phone call from a friend of mine who told me about someone who needed a caterer for an event. And that was it. I knew at that moment I got the answer to my question, and two days later I enrolled into culinary school." Chef had a few books in his hands that he gathered from the nightstand, and began returning them to their homes in the bookshelf.

"What made you step away from Christianity, if you don't mind me asking?" Paola wondered out loud. She comes from a very religious Catholic family, and completely shocked them when she made the decision a few years ago to step away from the establishment of the church to pursue a personal journey of spirituality. In her family, religious principles and traditions were as important as breathing. So when she announced her decision, it became yet another reason for her parents to blame Miguel for the way her life turned out.

"Enlightenment," Chef said with reassurance in his voice. "I started to question everything that I had been taught. I wanted to know why things had to be taken at face value, and why those who questioned the way things had always been were labeled as being of lesser faith, or worse, having doubt."

Paola let out a deep breath, with tears pooling in her hazel eyes. She understood exactly where Chef was coming from, and wished for the courage to explain her thoughts and feelings on the matter to her parents in the concise way that he did. "I wanted to know why certain things were demonized," he went on. "Like Buddhist teachings, and tarot, and why some members of the church claimed to believe in this almighty, all-loving, all consuming massive God, and yet so many of them lived very small lives with very little love in them. It didn't make sense to me that there were religions that were traced before Christianity, and yet it was the only acceptable belief system. I used to simply believe in God, but not anymore. Now, I KNOW God deeply and we have a very close relationship that affects every part of my life. It just doesn't look the way most people are told that it should look. And I'm okay with that. "

She paused to let his words sink into her mind. "That's major. What was that process like for you?" she asked. "It was beautiful. Intense and eye-opening for sure, but also very humbling. I was like a big skein of tangled yarn, and unlearning much of what had been my default setting for nearly thirty years was like unraveling that yarn bit by bit. When you become enlightened by things that contradict everything you've known to be true, it can be jarring. But if someone has gotten to this point in their journey, then they likely have a solid grip on who they are as a person, and that helps a lot. Knowing that you're resolved within yourself and firm in your beliefs of what you know to be true is all that matters."

Among Chef's collection of books is a tattered copy of 'Beyond Good and Evil' by Freidrich Nietzsche. Likely required reading for a philosophy course during his short lived college career. Dani picked up the book and started to thumb through it. "What college did you go to, Chef?" she asked him. "I attended community college for one semester, and never looked back!", he responded proudly. When he and I were getting to know each other, one of our first conversations was about school, and how neither one of us graduated from a four-year college, but not for lack of trying. I liked that he was proud of the fact that he knew himself well enough to know that the traditional education system wasn't for him.

"Really?" she asked. " I thought you had to go to an undergraduate program before going to culinary school in the United States." "Nope!" he said quickly. "I went to culinary school and did extremely well. The four-year traditional college route just wasn't for me though. I wasn't one of those kids in high school that excelled in their classes. I was usually bored, or tired from working and all I wanted to do was play basketball and video games. I gave college a shot though!"

"How did you know the traditional route for school wasn't going to work out for you?" Dani asked. "I had a sociology professor who told me that humans are not instinctive, but only reactive. I said that instinctive and reactive are two different things and he didn't agree. He refused any type of discourse, and I knew right then that I wouldn't be able to learn from someone who was so shortsighted. So I left and that was it. I went right back to working full time. Plus I had to drive an hour each way from Katy to San Jacinto, every day in Houston rush hour traffic."

His deep curiosity about endless topics has made him a student of life, though. He's always reading something, or watching a lecture, or listening to an old recording of a wise speaker and applying what resonates to his life.

Tory made his way from the lounge area of the bedroom over to us when he heard the topic of conversation. Much like his brother, the high school to four-year college pipeline wasn't a fit for him either. "My friends and I were just talking about this!" he said with the same intensity as Chef. "College is legit not for everyone, but we were all told that it was the only way to make money and be successful in our careers. That narrative worked for previous generations, and I think it's still profitable for some people today. But I really believe that the primary goal for getting people to go to college is to keep capitalism alive." Chef smiled at him with pride and agreed. "A lot of the constructs in American society are there for reasons other than what is shown on the surface. We all know that America runs on capitalism."

"Hell yeah it does!" Tory hollered, making the rest of us laugh. "It's woven into the fabric of everything. Baby Boomers were told that the American Dream was to graduate high school, enlist in the army or go to college, get a degree in a reputable major and get a good job. Start a family, stay at that job for forty to fifty years. Rinse and repeat."

"I would go so far as to say that the idea and construct isn't only limited to America," Paola started. "It's pretty much a common theme in most countries, and that same rhetoric was forced on Generation X, and for the most part it worked out well for them. Until millennials came along, and started to challenge the system. They aren't having as many kids or nearly as quickly as Gen X and Boomers did, which means we aren't producing as many laborers to keep the wheels turning in traditional jobs."

"You get it! Always ask questions. Always dig deeper and look beneath the surface" Chef exclaimed.

Our conversation was cut short by the sound of glass shattering on the kitchen floor. "I think that's my cue to get dinner served," Chef said with a laugh. "Good," Miguel said. "Because I finished my last egg roll when we were in the office and I'm hungry."

Chef led us out of the bedroom and into the hallway toward the front of the house. From where we're standing, every part of the house that we've walked through up to this point looks different now. The view of the foyer is much more clear. Candles, figurines and hourglasses that we initially didn't understand now have better meaning. The once colossal chandelier appears to have taken a different shape; still vibrant and bright but on a much smaller scale now.

"Do ya'll see that?" Lucas asked the rest of us. "It's wild right?" I added. "Everything changes shape and size the further we get away from it. It reminds me of that scene in Willy Wonka and the Chocolate Factory, when the parents and kids were walking to the other side of the hall, and it looked like they were growing and everything else was shrinking."

When he was designing the floorplan, Chef wanted the front of the house to appear different when the viewer was facing it from the back of the house. He wanted it to be symbolic of the way our fears and perspectives on life tend to look differently as we grow and progress. Maturity and the passing of time are not synonymous. People can go through life and have the exact same mindset as they did twenty years prior. Growth and maturity are choices. Choosing to grow and work on your vulnerability and humility breaks down the ego, and helps us to keep it in check. When we truly commit to the work of becoming a more evolved version of yourself, everything that brought us to that point looks differently than it did before. Arguments, frustrations, fears, connections, and mental blocks serve as stepping stones that guide you to where you were always supposed to be. Just as significant, but smaller and not as scary or intimidating.

—

My father never knew his father, and from my perspective he never wanted to know him. He was absent, and my father hated him for it! His younger self expressed to me that if he ever met his dad he would punch him in the face because he was never there for him, "so fuck him!" Many years later, that wounded child inside of him sought out healing and went on a major search for my grandfather. With new technologies like Ansestory.com, 23andMe.com, and other DNA family finder sites, my father dove head first into all of them and along the way he got me to send my DNA to these institutions as well. To be honest, this search for my long lost family that I never knew didn't interest me in the slightest. My perspective is that the Universe, the Cosmos, God, Allah, or whatever your religion subscribes to, set up everything perfectly including my grandfather. Ervin Victor Green (Pop), fell deeply in love with my biological paternal grandmother and later married her. Taking on all of her family responsibilities like raising a family, and I personally don't believe there could have been a better person for the job. So I personally didn't have a void to fill or any healing to do around the matter. Pop is my grandfather and I'm cool with that, however nearsighted that perspective was at the time.

After the results of the DNA testing came back, my father and I learned that this lost grandfather of mine, Frank Johnson, was a career chef in the military and worked for several years as a cook in Nevada. Here it is, both my father and I are deeply influenced by culinary and the direct contact from my grandfather was missing the entire time. The power of DNA passing along critical talents and information that jumps over physical barriers like absent fathers is incredibly impressive, and leads me to wonder what else has been passed along that I'm not aware of.

With DNA analysis and research information from these institutions, sometimes you come across interesting passive information. There was a specific paternal lineage link on 23andME connecting the Pharaoh Ramses the 4th of ancient Kemet to myself through my father, from his father. So it would seem that this Frank Johnson guy carried some unique blood, with deep ties and a meaningful impact on my life.

This very interesting information coincided with a book that I happened to read about a year earlier called God Wills The Negro by Theodore P. Ford. It was a deep study of the southern blacks in America around the early 1900's, and their religious and spiritual practices. The culture of southern blacks at that time was well preserved because the deep south didn't integrate their slaves, which caused them to sneak off in the night to continue their spiritual traditions from Africa. With the northern slaves' culture being erased by integration, Sir Theodore P. Ford was heavily interested in the ancient spiritual practices of the Kemetic high priests and the traditions they set forth. His book lays out the specifics of the different types of African slaves and which region of the USA they were shipped to. Pointing out that the fleeing Keminites were later captured by European forces west of Kush, who then shipped them to the regions later known as the Bible Belt of America. Kemet which is what the Egyptians called themselves, had royal families that were sold into slavery by their African kin in frear of being enslaved themselves. A lot of the families that landed in Louisiana were of a Pharaonic descent according to his research.

I was a child of many questions! My mother encouraged it, and my gullible nature took it and ran to the moon. This applied to religion and the Christan church which didn't like all of those questions, they wanted you to sit there and take it. Being the strong willed person that I am, if I have a question I'm going to get answers one way or another. It was an innocent search because I felt lost and the notion that this savior in a fiery chariot was going to swoop down from the clouds and save little 'ole me just wasn't comforting. God hates jealousy yet God is a jealous God and you shall not put anything before him. Okay , if you say so.. but love isn't jealous.

The one thing that was burning in the side of my head since childhood was the witch hunts of Salem, Massachusetts, because we all know witches aren't real right? No broom sticks or boiling brews, no green faces and crackling laughs, right? So why did so many people die behind something that wasn't real? That led me into rooms that Christanity forbade me to enter, because the Father that loves me will ship me off to burn for eternity. Anything dealing with witches and magic was labeled as devilish and something people should stay away from. That's when the naive blinders over my eyes began to crack, and I started reading book after book on the occult. I thought at one point that the word Occult referred to the devil, however it just means "that which is hidden".

Now this is all coming from someone who failed 7th grade English, and always read multiple years behind their grade level in school. I would always pass when it was my turn to read out loud in classrooms, and to put it simply, words have always been my kryptonite. However, when I came across this information about the ancient world and how it operated, I just couldn't get enough of it. It answered just about every question I ever had about spiritual Godly connections and what went on in the world. Alchemy, Herbalism, Chakras, Spirits, Energies & Aurus, Rituals, Spells, Astrology, Numerology and Ancient Shamanic Practices were all labeled as demonic yet this is what the high priest of my ancestors knew and practiced for tens of thousands of years. This information took me from fearing God & the Devil, to knowing and understanding them which liberaterated me from fear!

The truth of a lot of this information is hard to take at times, because most people stay within the boundaries that their parents and grandparents set for them. I've learned that to find true knowledge, you must travel well beyond your comfort zone. The funny thing is that you will travel quite a ways to realize that you are searching for yourself, because all of the universe is inside of your soul. So there it is, if you were searching for the all mighty truth about all there is and that will be, Its You, your Soul which is a sun just like the sun & the stars!
-Kababo

Chapter 8

Kababo Dumpling

In the ghettos of America like the one I was raised in, you'll often meet people that haven't ventured very far from where they were raised. At one point, I thought that thinking that way was only something poor people dealt with. Until I was the Executive Chef at Bay Oaks Country Club in Clear Lake Houston Texas, and met wealthy old money with the same condition, never venturing far from where they were raised. Some of the people I met had never left Clear Lake in their entire life, unless it was for a vacation for a short period of time. The only interaction each of those sections of society have with each other is through TV & the Internet. This ignorance leads to a ton of fear within these groups and even more misconceptions about the other. Much like laughter, cooking is universal, and no matter which group you belong to, you know when food is good.
-Kababo

With every step we made closer to the kitchen, the effervescent scent of garlic and onion, and something sweet and floral grew stronger. Chef hadn't told us about the menu for tonight, it didn't matter. Whatever he was serving, we were already hungry for it.

The long rectangular dining table is expertly set with a white linen tablecloth and white dinnerware with black and gold trim. Tea lights are scattered across the center of the table, and four bouquets of the same bright orange and pink flowers and greenery from the backyard are neatly placed in square vases. Just high enough for us to see each other across the table. We all took our seats at our assigned chairs, marked by place cards with the signature Chef Kababo & Co. logo. Chef knew to sit Paola and Miguel across from one another for obvious reasons, and had Tory next to Paola, and me

between him and Kamryn, and Mr. Cardenas next to Miguel.

"Alright, everyone," Chef announced. "As I mentioned earlier in the evening,

tonight's meal will be full of tasty surprises." Just then, Lucas and Dani brought around

the first course on crystal serving trays. Chef stood at the head of the table with his

white kitchen towel still folded into his front pocket as he presented the dish to us.

"What we have first is the Kababo Dumpling. It's a fusion of Indian and Asian elements

with a bit of my personality on a plate. It's bold, bright, and flavorful and if you don't want

more I didn't do my job right."

I recognize the distinct savory aroma of the dumplings before I take a bite. The

blend of spices & herbs takes me back to one night in Houston. It was late, and I was

sitting at one of the two desks in his apartment that served as an on-site office for Chef

Kababo and Co. I was knee-deep in an op-ed for The New York Times. While he sat at

his, taking puffs from a joint and checking his stocks. He must have noticed that I hadn't

taken a break to eat, because I heard him in the tiny kitchen with sizzling pans and the

sound of his blade slicing through vegetables. The next thing I knew, he was walking

toward me with a forkful of something. I tilted my chin up to him and opened my mouth,

and let the bite dance and melt on my tongue. It was amazing! Before I could get the

words out to ask what he just gave me, he was already smirking and padding back

toward the kitchen to finish up. "And they're not even done yet!". That was enough to

get my attention and make me realize that I was hungry after all. I got up from the desk and followed him to the kitchen, and watched as he carefully spooned the perfect amount of filling onto the dumpling wrapper before using his long fingers to delicately fold the edges like they were two-bite sized Christmas packages. As if he had done it a million times, and could do it with his eyes closed. He dropped the wrapped and filled dumplings into the shallow pan of hot oil, and proceeded to flip them over when they were the perfect golden brown. He placed a few of the dumplings on a dinner plate, grabbed a squeeze bottle filled with some sort of sauce and drizzled it alongside them. "Go sit down, I'll bring it to you", he said. So I sat cross legged on his pull out couch, and he brought the plate and two glasses of wine to me. We sat there together, laughing and talking about everything and nothing in between bites of dumpling and sips of red wine. If I remember correctly, that's the night he told me about his plans for Costa Rica, and how he was surprised that he had so quickly reached a point in his career where he had to turn down clients after wanting them for so long.

It's nice to see everyone enjoying their dumplings and hearing them trade guesses about the ingredients. Tory is certain that he makes better dumplings than his big brother, and Dani is convinced that there's some sort of mint stuffed inside them. I think that's part of the process that Chef enjoys too. He doesn't necessarily put a lot of stock in what people say about his food. Watching how they respond to his food, especially if they ask for seconds or finish the meal entirely, gives him all the validation he needs.

Miguel has already cleaned his plate and motions to the waiter asking for seconds. "Do you plan on sharing some of your culinary secrets with us this evening,

Chef?", he hollers to the kitchen. Chef poked his head around the corner,"I don't know about all that, but if you guess correctly I might tell you that you're not wrong."

"I bet Kamryn knows what's in them", Paola hinted as she peered over the top of her glass of wine. A sneaky but sweet smile slowly spread across Kamryn's face. The same smile her dad has when he knows something that others don't. "It's possible!", she says, making the whole table laugh.

Jazz and soul music plays in the dining room as we savor our dumplings and sip red wine. The conversation is mellow and easy with the exception of the occasional burst of laughter until Miguel politely interjected, asking how we all were connected to Chef. "I'll start!", Tory announced to the table, proudly. "He's been my big brother for about twenty one years, and he never cooks for me." Chef shouted from the kitchen, "That's because I taught your ass how to cook so I wouldn't have to!". Lucas was standing near the entry to the kitchen with a pitcher of water, when he let out a belly laugh, making the rest of us laugh with him. He noticed the way Chef treated his brother was the same way she treated him, with strong guidance and a tendency to poke fun at him. As Chef's protege, Lucas gets a lot of professional and personal advice from him almost every day.

"I'll go next," Lucas said as he walked around the table to refill our water glasses. "About a year ago, I read in the paper that there was a free two-day culinary clinic being offered by a Chef from the U.S. so I decided to check it out. When I got there, it was me and like six other people, and I was kind of intimidated because they were all really talented and were already working as chefs and cooks at major restaurants in town. Everything I knew about cooking came from my grandma, and it wasn't technical or anything, but she was the best cook in our town so I thought it counted for something. During the class, everyone was moving faster than I was and that made me a little self conscious, but it kind of worked out because I was the only one in the class that spoke English so I stood out. We got to talking a lot about food during the clinic, and he told me about his bed and breakfast and everything. On the last day of the clinic when everybody was leaving, I went up to him and asked if he needed any help at the bed and breakfast because I was looking for a job and wanted to get better at cooking. He agreed to let me come out to the property a couple days out of the week to help him with prep work, and now I'm his right hand and sous chef." Lucas was proud to learn from him and even more proud to be trusted enough to work alongside him. Chef was happy to have the extra help in the kitchen when he was establishing the menu and getting his bearings in the city, but it means more to him to be able to pass along the knowledge and patience that his own mentors had for him.

Dani picked up where Lucas left off in his story. "I used to drop Lucas off here at the property for work, and one day when he was getting out of the car he needed my help to carry some fruit inside the work kitchen. I walked into the kitchen and saw this tall guy with a beard standing at the counter holding his cell phone up to his ear.. He looked really frustrated, and then I noticed his laptop was in front of him, and he was trying to use Google translate to help him explain to whoever he was talking to that he needed to place an order for towels and linens. I walked up to him and asked if I could help him, and I remember he looked at me all shocked and surprised that I would approach him like that. I told him that I was obviously fluent in English and Spanish, and asked him to tell me what he wanted. I took the phone and easily told the other person what he needed. I had my brother Lucas bring me a pen and some paper and I wrote down all the important information and had him write down the address. When I was done, I gave him the phone back and told him that he could pay me at the end of the week! I was messing around, but he asked me if I had a job and if I had any experience in management. I told him that I'm the oldest daughter, and already working and maintaining our household pretty much on my own since our parents are always working really hard. We talked about pay and hours, and what I wanted to learn and the next thing I knew I had a job."

Next up was Paola. She's one of the most beautiful people I've ever met. She has a quiet strength about her that precedes her the moment she walks into any room, and she has a way of making whoever she's talking to feel like they are the only person on the planet. Her piercing green eyes and warm, friendly smile makes everyone feel at home, especially when she speaks of her beloved homeland, Brazil. She's a sociology professor with a love for travel, music and the arts, and an ideal complement to Miguel's boisterous personality. The two are just as in love today as they were when they got married many years ago. If you're ever in a crowded room with them, you can always find them tucked away in a corner somewhere, gazing into each other's eyes and one of them with their hand lovingly placed on the others' cheek. They're the best of friends. Inseparable.

"Let's see. How did I meet the famous Chef Kababo.", she ponders aloud in her thick Portuguese accent. "Well, one evening, my husband Miguel and I were at a really fancy dinner party for one of his clients. The cocktail hour conversation was really pretentious and boring, so we snuck away to the kitchen to see what we could find to nibble on. When we walked in, we saw this tall, bearded guy with an apron giving out instructions to the staff. But we couldn't tell if he was the head chef in charge, or a part of the serving team because he was so involved with everything going on. We watched him move from the stove to the sink to washing dishes." Miguel nodded his head at the memory. "That's right!" he said. "He noticed we were standing there and jokingly asked if we were having fun. He knew the party was dry and could tell that they weren't our type of crowd. We laughed and started talking about the menu - braised short ribs with whipped feta mashed potatoes, but he brought some of what he and the staff were snacking on. Peach bruschetta with goat cheese, basil and infused honey." Paola closed her eyes and shook her head from side to side, as if to conjure the taste from her memory. "I'll never forget it, " she said. "It was such a simple appetizer, but together it was just out of this world! We started talking about where he was from and how he got to Costa Rica, and we told him about the flower shop and how we knew the host. From then on, it felt like the three of us had been friends for years. Which is pretty rare for us, since we're not everyone's cup of tea." Paola smirked and glanced in Cardenas' direction, making Kamryn laugh out loud.

"That next week I made a big dinner for our family and we invited Chef Kababo over to the house so that he could enjoy a nice home cooked meal. Now for us, the meal was a normal dish for our family. Lots of fresh ingredients, bold flavors and good quality meat and fish. But I was unsure if he would be comfortable with this kind of cuisine, so I had also included some more American food like potatoes and chicken. And I noticed that he was eating more of our traditional food, and I loved that. He wasn't afraid to try new things like feijoada, which is a Brazilian stew that my mother and grandmothers would make when I was growing up. We talked all night about cooking, and spices, and traveling, and goals and all kinds of things that would normally take new friends years to talk about."

The conversation moved to Miguel sharing about his childhood growing up in Costa Rica, and how he experienced a lot of the indigenious cultures for most of his life, but didn't have much interaction with other cultures until he was much older. "You'll see some people here of African or Caribbean descent, but that's pretty much it. It wasn't until I traveled to the U.S. in my early twenties that I really got to see people of other backgrounds that also spoke Spanish but looked nothing like me. I would go to New York and spend summers with my cousins and friends of the family, and I remember how much I loved the city and how vibrant and loud it was and how the people there were just as vibrant. Everything and everyone moved so quickly, as if there was something important happening at a particular time that no one could be late for. But it would just be people going to the grocery store or running errands or something."

"That's exactly how I felt when I visited. It was crazy to me that there were people who looked Black or African but were fluent in Spanish and were Dominican or Puerto Rican. Everybody was always in a hurry, and they could tell if you were a tourist or not from there just by how you walked, approached the subway, or ordered your food at a bodega."

That's one thing that I love about Africans and the entire diaspora of Black people. We aren't a monolith. We exist in so many spaces, and most of them are completely different from what are depicted in movies and media. Our lineage is so vast, and most of it can be traced back to the exact villages and tribes that our ancestors belonged to.

"So Chef, now that you've had a chance to experience Costa Rica as more than just a tourist, and now a resident, how do you like it here?" Paola asked him. "I love it here! There's so many things about it that made me want to move here and bring my business with me, but for the most part is the peace of mind that I feel when I'm here. Not to say that I didn't have that back home. Don't get me wrong, I'm a Houston guy, born and raised and proud of it! But there's just so much more of the world to see than my city, and even the country."

"That's incredible to me", Dani said with her mouth half full. "I love Costa Rica too, and my family was all born and raised here for several generations, but most of us have never even left the country. I don't know that I could leave here for more than a few months for vacation or study or something like that."

"That's totally understandable! Most people don't leave their home state or even their own city, and I think it has to do with access and sight. If you come from a family that doesn't travel much, or fear may play a major role in the fabric of the family dynamic, it can be hard to even see yourself leaving your city. Some of my relatives have never left Houston, and a lot of my friends that I grew up with never left Greenspoint."

"How did your family react when you told them that you wanted to visit other countries?" Dani asked. "A lot of them were shocked! They warned me about not knowing or understanding the culture in Europe, and they worried that I didn't know the language and that the customs were completely different from in the States. But I went anyway. They definitely supported me and eventually came around to the idea after I had been gone a little while, but it took them some time. From my experience, people will project their own fears and insecurities onto you if you let them. Like I said, no one in my family up to that point had ever been out of the country, so they could only relate to me from their point of reference. Which is fine, but I think anyone in the position that I was in should take it all with a grain of salt. Do your own research. Watch documentaries about the places that you want to visit, and get acquainted with the culture. And when you get there, experience everything that you can. Soak up the culture, immerse yourself in everything that the location has to offer, and more than anything else - eat the food!"

"Of all of the places that you've traveled to, how did you know that you wanted to move here?" Paola asked. Having seen most of the world by the time she was in her late twenties, Paola had fallen in love with many cities. Morocco, Mexico City, São Paulo and Phuket all had a piece of her heart and a past lover or three, but nothing felt quite as perfect to her as Costa Rica.

"The first time that I visited, I really loved how beautiful it was," Chef added. "The climate was tropical and amazing, and I learned that it made for the perfect environment for growing organic herbs, fruits and vegetables in a way that wasn't possible back home. That was a major green light for me too, because a big part of my culinary journey has been focused on health and wellness. I've always wanted to grow and cook food that was nutrient dense and beneficial to the body. A lot of western foods are absolutely terrible because they are grown and manufactured with the idea of mass consumption in mind, and not about nutritional value."

"I hear you talk about that all the time!" Miguel said with his mouth full. "I can't believe some of the things that are allowed in grocery stores and even given to kids."

"It's the truth! When I was in Europe I was shocked when I went to the grocery stores, and couldn't find things that were so readily available in the U.S. There was a section of the store called "American Foods", and it had random shit like Pop-Tarts, granola, cereal, and peanut butter. It blew my mind! So of course, I'm always wanting to learn more about things. I researched it and found out that there's a very long list of chemicals and ingredients that are harmful to people that are in many everyday, common pantry staples. You won't find frozen waffles or brightly colored chips, cereal, sodas and candies like you do in America. All that stuff is trash and causes all kinds of health problems, and the government knows about it! Yet, it's advertised to kids and marketed as delicious. Don't get me wrong, I grew up on a lot of that stuff, and will rarely if ever turn down a Double Stuffed Oreo. But health is wealth, man. I tell that to my family, my friends, and anyone that I have a connection with. Taking care of your body is essential to a healthy life, and it all starts with what you eat. I don't want to be an old man needing oxygen or having all kinds of health problems. That seems terrible to me. I want to be in my 60s and 70s still thriving and enjoying the fruits of my labor with as little inflammation in my body as possible. So, that tea that you all had earlier this evening is the product of one of my health concerns. I had just had major surgery and was constantly taking ibuprofen to keep the inflammation down. Shortly after that, I was diagnosed with stress ulcers, so the 2000 mg to 3000 mg of Ibuprofen that I was taking each day for my back pain definitely didn't help my stomach. I was convinced that there was a natural way to heal myself through what I consumed. I refused to take medication that would compromise my kidneys and liver. A lot of the medication that we are prescribed is damaging and has many adverse effects on the body, but that's a different story for another time. At that time though, I knew that fruit and natural herbs have healing properties, so again, I did a ton of research and formulated this tea that would promote anti-inflammation. The tea took about a month to really work, and it definitely wasn't a quick fix. But it was a permanent one. I don't have to keep relying on it the same way that I would have had to take a pill every day. Now, if I feel any sort of inflammation , I know that I can treat it with my tea. But slowly over time, I began to heal. I drank multiple cups every day, that totalled about two liters. Since then, I've played around with the ingredients and ratios, and have gotten it down to a pretty precise recipe. So any time someone has inflamation, that tea will definitely help."

"I love that you take natural remedies to heal and maintain your physical health. That's something that my family has done for generations back in Brazil", Paola said. "Some of it was due to the fact that it was expensive to see a doctor, but it was largely because there are better ways to heal the body than to pump it with unnatural medicines."

"Yeah for sure. That's how it should be, in my opinion" Chef added. "We should always reach for natural ingredients that come from the Earth before we decide to put something else in our bodies. Don't get me wrong, I definitely believe in science, and I know that scientific advancements are what made it possible for us to have antibiotics and other cures. I just prefer holistic medicine over western medicine that tends to medicate rather than heal."

The conversation was halted by the sight of Chef's service staff holding trays of our next course. As invested as we all were in the *discourse*, we couldn't help but to be intrigued by what was coming next.

NET WT. 15 OZ.

Chef's Tea

My 5th lumbar had a 7x13 mm fragment on the left side and the pain was excruciating! During the process of doctor visits, physical therapy, more doctor visits, and finally surgery, I became accustomed to taking 3000 mg of Ibuprofen per day to keep the inflammation down. I'm not one for taking a lot of medications, so this couldn't have been the final solution for my pain. If I listened to the doctors, steroid injections on some semi-annual basis to keep their pockets padded while I suffered in pain would have been the remedy. Of the three doctors I saw, the third didn't even know I had a fragment in my back and had a shocked look on his face after I asked him to review my chart. To say the least, I'm not the most trusting of doctor's recommendations simply because they suggest it. After the successful surgery, I had to find a more permanent solution to the chronic inflammation that didn't include pills and doctors. After researching natural remedies for anti-inflammation, I came up with a really good mix to make a daily tea. Since I have access to a commercial kitchen to test out different mixes, I was able to get the balance right and now I'm happy to share with you a recipe that changed my life. Drinking this tea daily has removed the need for Ibuprofen, and I have absolutely no back pain. I still drink this daily, heck I'm sipping on some right now as I type this. I hope it helps you out with your inflammation.

Ingredients

Fresh Ginger Root - 1 #

Fresh Turmeric - 1 #

Pineapple - 1 #

Chamomile - ¼ #

Burdock Root - ¼ #

Dandelion Root - ¼ #

Elderberry - ¼ #

Honey - 1 c (optional)

Tools

1 medium - large pot (8 qt) ish

1 Strainer

Time: 1 hour

Peel the skin off of the Ginger root before cutting it into chunks, the skin is bitter and has a lot of tannins. Using a spoon firmly scrape the skin off of the ginger. It's best if you can peel & cut your fresh Turmeric into chunks as well but that can be a bit more tedious than the Ginger. Buy a whole pineapple and only use the skins in the tea while you eat the yummy fruit. We only want the flavor of pineapple and the skins deliver on that perfectly so you don't have to waste the whole fruit. Discard the top and bottom of the pineapple because they hold a lot of dirt and grit, only use the sides of the skins, and make sure you wash them well. You can order Burdock Root (cut), Dandelion Root (cut), & Elderberry from an online herb distributor like the one that I use, essentialorganicingredients.com. Once all of your items are into the pot you can fill it with water 1 inch from the top. Turn your heat on medium and allow the water to come up to temperature. If you want to use honey, this is the perfect time for you to add it to the pot. All of the items will float at the top of your pot at the start of this process but when they fall to the bottom is when you know it is time to turn the heat off and allow for the ingredients to steep for about 30 additional mins. At this point use your strainer and seperate the lovely tea from the ingredients and drink up!!

KABABQ

<u>Kababo Lore</u>

In an age when the ways and rules of the universe are controlled by tyrannical powers with the intent to control and oppress those under their rule, the etheric moon dragon, Kababo emerges from his shell. Despite having been surrounded by oppressive energy since conception, The Kababo triples in size and strength with each passing day, developing an insatiable appetite to subjugate the very energies that seek to overtake the universe. Ultimately, liberating all living things from forces carrying the intention of crushing others beneath their weight. Within The Kababo lies the balance of the feminine and the masculine, the giver and the receiver, the delicate and the indestructible. The Kababo dumpling is a tactile representation of the all encompassing force that seeks to eradicate oppression, by subjecting it to its own powers.

The age of slumber has ended, time has ripened the air for the birth of something new from something very old. These Dragon Eggs were thought to be fossils all across the earth from a very distant past. Until an excavation team, Chef Penright & Co. unearthed the mother load of Dragon Eggs in Acres Homes Houston, Texas. There were so many, the team started experimenting on ways to use them. Naturally, cooking them came to mind, and when it did…the results were explosive!

Kababo Dumplings

Ingredients

Chicken Breast - 454 g (1 pound)

Plain Yogurt - 454 g (1 pound)

Cream Cheese - 454 g (1 pound)

Roasted Coriander - 28 g (2 tbsp)

Roasted Cumin - 28 g (2 tbsp)

Smoked Paprika - 28 g (2 tbsp)

Dark Chili Powder - 28 g (2 tbsp)

Roasted Fennel Seeds - 14 g (1 tbsp)

Turmeric Powder - 28 g (2 tbsp)

Ginger Powder - 14 g (1 tbsp)

Coarse Ground Black Pepper - 14 g (1 tbsp)

Minced Serrano Peppers - 2 whole

Butter - 454 g (1 pound)

Coarse Kosher Salt - 28 g (2 tbsp)

Fresh Mint - 454 g (1 pound)

Fresh Ginger (Peeled) - 454 g (1 pound)

Pistachios - 52 g

Lemon Juice - 2 whole lemons

Coarse Kosher Salt - 14 g

Extra Virgin Olive Oil - 237 ml

Korean Wheat Flour - 2 c (not whole wheat flour)

Corn Starch - 2 c

Salt - 2 tbsp

Water - 2 c

Vegetable Oil - ¼ inch deep in pan

Chili Paste - 42 ml (3 tbsp)

Tools

Blender
Sheet Pan
Medium Sautee Pan
Medium Sauce Pot
Tupperware
Medium Mixing Bowl
Food Processor (Optional)
Parchment Paper

Kababo Dumpling Filling

Ingredients

Chicken Breast - 454 g (1 pound)
Plain Yogurt - 454 g (1 pound)
Cream Cheese - 454 g (1 pound)
Roasted Coriander - 28 g (2 tbsp)
Roasted Cumin - 28 g (2 tbsp)
Roasted Fennel Seeds - 28 g (2 tbsp)
Smoked Paprika - 28 g (2 tbsp)
Dark Chili Powder - 28 g (2 tbsp)
Roasted Fennel Seeds - 14 g (1 tbsp)
Turmeric Powder - 28 g (2 tbsp)
Ginger Powder - 14 g (1 tbsp)
Coarse Ground Black Pepper - 14 g (1 tbsp)
Minced Serrano Peppers - 2 whole
Butter - 454 g (1 pound)
Coarse Kosher Salt - 28 g (2 tbsp)

Tools

Blender
Sheet Pan
Medium Sautee Pan
Medium Saucepan

You aren't going to find roasted coriander, cumin, or fennel seeds in the store so you will have to do it yourself, and the flavor reward will be totally worth it. Purchase these 3 items whole and roast them in the oven for 15 - 20 mins on 350 degrees F. If you want to make a small batch of each to save some for later you want to roast them on different sheet pans but if you are only making enough for this recipe then 1 sheet pan will work just fine. You can also roast these on the stove top in a sautee pan over medium / medium high heat for about 5 - 7 mins, while tossing the spices in the pan to prevent burning. If you notice the edges of the spices are turning black it's time to take them out of the oven and or off the stove top. Once they are roasted you will place them into a blender or coffee grinder to make them into a powder.

Allow your cream cheese to sit out at room temperature.

Now let's marinade the chicken with the Spiced Ghee Cream Cheese. To make the ghee you will place the 454 g of butter into a small sauce pot and set the flame to medium heat. Clarifying butter takes some time (30 - 45 mins) and you don't want the butter to hard boil at any point. If you notice the boiling is aggressive, turn your flame down a bit to adjust for this. However you do want it to lightly boil, so if the flame is not producing any bubbles within the melted butter crank your flame up a bit. Every stove top is different so I can't simply say turn yours on 5 and everything will be fine. With advanced culinary you are always watching, smelling, hearing, touching, & tasting your food along the way to ensure its bomb! Your butter will create a white foamy layer across the top of the liquid, when this foamy layer falls to the bottom of the pot it's finished. I would like to reiterate that if your flame is too high you will have brown clarified butter, which is a thing but not the thing we are looking for. Take a strainer and separate the yummy golden ghee from the fat solids at the bottom of the pot.

Now you have your ghee (which is also clarified butter).Use a medium mixing bowl add the cream cheese, plain yogurt, and all of your spices along with your minced serrano peppers (chop very finely).

Roasted Coriander - 28 g (2 tbsp)
Roasted Cumin - 28 g (2 tbsp)
Roasted Fennel Seeds - 28 g (2 tbsp)
Smoked Paprika - 28 g (2 tbsp)
Dark Chili Powder - 28 g (2 tbsp)
Roasted Fennel Seeds - 14 g (1 tbsp)
Turmeric Powder - 28 g (2 tbsp)
Ginger Powder - 14 g (1 tbsp)
Coarse Ground Black Pepper - 14 g (1 tbsp)
Minced Serrano Peppers - 2 whole

Slowly pour in the ghee and mix all together. The texture should be soft and creamy. The ghee should be warm when pouring into the mixing bowl.

Take a portion of this Spiced Ghee Cream Cheese and completely slather the chicken breast and allow it to marinate for 24 hours. If you would prefer to do everything in one day you can marinate the chicken in the morning and cook it that evening, however for a better taste allow it to sit overnight in the marinade. Use only enough to cover the chicken in a thin layer.

After your chicken breast has sat for a day it's time to cook it. Adjust your stove top flame to medium-high and place a medium sized sautee pan onto the flame. Allow your pan to fully come up to temperature before placing 14 g (1 tbsp) of butter inside of the pan. The purpose of searing is to caramelize the outer part of the item (in this case a chicken breast) to lock in moisture and flavor. You will sear the chicken breast on each side on the stove top. Once both sides are seared you will adjust the flame down to medium heat and allow the chicken to simmer to completion, please note if your chicken breast is getting dry add some more butter, use 14 g (1 tbsp) at a time.

Hot pan > Butter > Sear chicken breast > Flip > Sear second side of chicken breast > adjust flame to medium heat and allow to simmer to completion, add additional butter during the simmering part if the chicken breast has absorbed all of the previous butter. You want to simmer both sides of the chicken breast to ensure even cooking. Some of you are looking for a time for each process however that is quite hard to do in this case, approximately this will take 10 mins.

Once your chicken is fully cooked you will mince the chicken breast with either a food processor or a chef knife. Take the minced chicken breast and fold into the Spiced Ghee Cream Cheese mix. This will complete your filling for the Kababo Dumplings!

Sauce

Ginger Mint Pesto

Fresh Mint - 454 g (1 pound)
Fresh Ginger (Peeled) - 454 g (1 pound)
Pistachios - 52 g
Lemon Juice - 2 whole lemons
Coarse Kosher Salt - 14 g
Extra Virgin Olive Oil - 237 ml

Tools

Blender
Table Spoon

Remove the Mint from the stems and place into a blender. Peel the Ginger with a table spoon and cut into large chunks then place into the blender along with the remaining ingredients. Blend until consistent and set aside for later.

Chili Paste

For the Chili Paste we are going to save a bit of time seeing this is already a complicated recipe, and there are several good quality brands out there. Each region of the world is different so choose your favorite brand of chili paste and roll with that one.

Dumpling Wrapper

Korean Wheat Flour - 2 c (not whole wheat flour, All Purpose flour can be substituted)
Corn Starch - 2 c
Salt - 2 tbsp
Water - 2 c

Tools

Mixer w/ Dough Hook (optional)
Rolling Pin
Parchment Paper or foil
Sheet Pan

Using a very similar recipe from the Filet Mignon Egg Rolls (refer to the recipe on page 39) except this time you are not rolling it paper so thin.

Grab a medium size mixing bowl and add your dry ingredients first, then add 1c of water to bring it all together.Stir with a wooden spoon or your hand, the point is to combine everything together so you can knead it for a bit, building up the strength within the dough. For a dumpling you are going to want the dough a bit thicker to provide some quality texture. Use flour/cornstarch mix to scatter some across your working surface, this is to prevent sticking. You will take 28 g (1 oz) of the dough and roll it in the palm of your hand until it's round and somewhat smooth. Using the palm of your hand you will press down on the dough against your work surface to flatten it out before using a rolling pin to form a flat round mini pizza. Make sure your rolling pin is floured to prevent the dough from sticking to the pin. Aim for 100 mm (4 inches) in diameter and you will be fine, if you go over a bit that's cool too. This isn't a science, it's an art!

Place each mini pizza-like dough piece onto a sheet pan with parchment paper or foil on the bottom and cover the top with another sheet of parchment paper. This will prevent the dough from drying out while you complete your other mini pizzas. Lightly scatter flour across the bottom sheet to prevent the dough from sticking. Once you have completed all of the dough rolling it's time to stuff the dumpling.

Use ½ tbsp of the filling and place in the center of the dough. You will fold the dough around the filling like a taco connecting the two opposite edges of dough together. Now this part is a bit tricky to describe, refer to www.chefpenright.com to watch a video of the recipe but more so to understand how to fold the dumplings. The portion of the dumpling that is away from you will remain flat, while making pinch pleats with the front side of the dough. Each fold will overlap the previous fold and work your way towards the edge. Start in the center of the dough taco and work down one side, once that side is complete return back to the middle and work down the other side. The extreme right and left ends of the dumpling will be tucked around the back of the dumpling to complete the process. Place each finished dumpling back onto the floured sheet pan with parchment paper and proceed to the next.

Now that the prepping is complete it's time to put some heat on these dumplings. So professionals use a dumpling pot, also known as a steamer. If you don't have one of those you can use the homely version of foil with small holes poked throughout. They basically work in the same fashion, one is more secure than the other. Using a little veggie oil or canola oil to base the bottom of the pot to prevent the dumplings from sticking. Cooking these is a 2 step process, first by steaming them for 7 minutes followed by shallow frying them for an additional 2 mins. Prepare a medium sauce pan and fill the bottom of the pan with 7mm (¼ inch) of canola oil and heat to 325 F or medium-high heat. Remember this isn't a science so don't attempt to follow this recipe step by step, inch by inch, you have to observe and make small adjustments along the way if you notice something burning or looking weird.

Use a spatula to gently raise the steamed dumplings from the steamer and place them into the frying pan. This will provide a lovely golden brown bottom on the dumpling and delivers an amazing crunchy texture to the dish.

Now it's time to plate up, if you are feeling artsy you can swoosh your sauces across your canvas (also known as a plate), but if you would like to play it safe you can place them into 2 separate ramekins for fun dipping. I would normally place 5 or 6 dumplings in a circle on top of the sauce "swooshes" and dig in, sloping up the sauces like biscuits and gravy. Enjoy!!

Chapter 9

Crab Cake Benny

The first time I left the United States was to work for the American Department of Defense in Iraq and that journey was so eye opening. For the first time in my life, I wasn't an African American! People in other countries didn't know what to think of me until I spoke to them and they heard my dialect. Some people thought I was Caribbean while others thought I was from Africa somewhere. All my life I was treated as an African American by the population of the United States, which we all know isn't the most celebrated group by any means. While in Iraq, I remember speaking with the locals and in a joking fashion they were telling me if the Taliban was to overrun the military camp just take my hair down (I had cornrows braids at the time) and come live with them because nobody would know the difference. They didn't have any beef with Africa and would most likely let me go free. For the first time, I wasn't the bad guy!
– Kababo

"This next dish is very special to me, and I'm pleased to share it with you all. I mentioned it earlier in the evening, but my father was also a chef, and so was his biological father before him. So I came into the profession pretty honestly, and I might go so far as to say it was destiny. Every Christmas morning, my father would make Eggs Benedict for our family, and it was my favorite thing in the whole world to eat. It's probably still my favorite. I would go to sleep on Christmas Eve with so much anticipation, just like every other kid, but it was mainly because I knew breakfast would be amazing. The hollandaise was silky and rich, and my father had it down to a science. I would watch him make it, and I was always fascinated by the way he could turn simple egg yolks into this perfect sauce. Later, I understood the process of whisking the yolks, and the important role that time and patience played in the process. So tonight, I want to share some of that with you in my Crab Cakes Benedict."

Kamryn and I immediately lit up and looked at each other with excitement. Crab Cakes Benedict is our favorite Chef Kababo signature dish to eat together. Chef carried on the tradition of making it for the family on Christmas, but every blue moon he likes to surprise us and make it for a late night dinner and invite his dad over to feast with us. His father once told me at a family gathering that it was always his favorite dish to make, and that he missed being able to cook for everyone on Christmas morning, so he appreciates that Chef has continued to make it so many years later. He also made it a point to tell me that a lot of restaurants make their hollandaise with cream cheese, which he thinks is terrible.

Dani walks around to each of us, and serves two piping hot eggs benedicts with jumbo lump crab cakes topped with a generous serving of creamy yellow hollandaise. Everyone immediately digs in, and Tory does a little shoulder shimmy in response to how tasty his first bite is.

"Chef, I never would have thought about making eggs benedict this way. The flavors are incredible!" Paola raved as she scooped a bite onto her fork and reached across the table to feed it to Miguel with a seductive wink.

"I'm really glad that you enjoy it. Traditional dishes like that are classics for a reason, but I think they can be sort of boring at times. I like to go against the grain, and do the unexpected when it comes to those old school type dishes," he said as he watched us savor each bite. "I love that approach," Dani said. "There's nothing worse than eating boring food. I hate it. It's like there's no life in it!" "I completely agree," Paola chimed in. "Food should be like sex. It should be wild and passionate, and never boring. Otherwise, you'll only be temporarily satisfied."

"Yes!" Dani said, her face all lit up with enthusiasm. "Good food should absolutely be like good sex. If it's bad, it's only memorable because of how terrible it was, right?" she asked for emphasis. "And if it's incredible," I started, "you're left thinking about it days or even weeks after. There's nothing like it, and nothing else to compare it to. Especially if it's incredible".

"Especially if it's incredible", Chef echoed with an eyebrow raised in intrigue as our eyes met. I bit my lower lip as I broke our gaze and went in for another bite of crab cake. "If you think about it, the only times when you are completely happy and in sheer bliss is when you're eating food and having sex", he said as he counted the instances with his index and middle fingers. "You know what, you're right,Chef!" Miguel said. "I never thought about it like that, but it's so true. And that's probably why it's so disappointing when something ruins either one of them."

"That's real! Amazing food and amazing sex are like religious experiences to me," Tory added. "K, remember when we watched that episode of Game of Thrones when that wedding happened?"

"The Red Wedding!" we all said in semi-unison. "Yes! Man, I know exactly where you're going. That's one of the main reasons why that episode was so powerful." Chef said. "Disrupting something so beautiful and sacred as the union of two people over a traditionally massive feast in such a violent way was complete sacrilege." "Exactly!" said Miguel. "Everyone at the wedding was relaxed and vulnerable and just enjoying themselves then BOOM. A massacre."

"Right! So I do my best to make sure that everything that I serve is an experience to be remembered, and without interruption if I can help it."

"Well everyone," Paola said as she raised her glass of wine. "Here's to always having incredible food and incredible sex!" We all raised our glasses and toasted in solidarity, before noticing Kamryn. "Yeah, I don't think I can legally toast to all of that just yet", she said with her eyes glued to her cell phone next to her place setting. "You're goddamned right!", her dad said with a deeper than usual tone, making us all laugh.

"Chef, I'm not sure about everyone else here, but I have to say that this evening's meal doesn't appear to be traditional or standard" Cardenas pointed out. "We haven't had an entree or a salad, or even bread for the table for that matter. It's been a few courses of appetizers, at best."

The lightheartedness in the room dissolved a bit and the tableside laughter grew silent, because for the most part, he was right. The meal has been anything but traditional, and nothing at all like what would be served at a restaurant. Paola and Miguel exchanged glances, and Kamryn and I locked eyes from across the table as she flashed me a surprised look without breaking stride in her meal. Chef stood next to my chair with his shoulders squared and arms crossed in front of him. "Mr. Cardenas, I'm so glad you pointed that out. That's exactly what I wanted to do with tonight's meal. To go against the grain, and present to you and my guests a culmination of flavors and experiences from my life. Everything that you have been served so far has been unorthodox in flavor profile and style, and I want it that way."

"So how do you possibly expect me to write a review of your meal when it doesn't qualify as a meal?" "That's where you're wrong," Chef said. "Just because my food doesn't fit into the boxes and definition of Michelin star restaurants and country club dining doesn't mean that it isn't a stellar meal. And we both know that I am beyond capable and equipped to make that type of food, because you've been to the establishments that I've built and cooked for. We've had several discussions about produce, and access to good quality ingredients back in Houston. So you'll be happy to know that each of the ingredients that you've tasted this evening were either locally grown, or grown right outside that door in my garden." He said, stretching his long arm and pointing toward the garden in the backyard. Cardenas had a puzzled look on his face and sat in silence for a beat. "Again, how do you possibly expect me to write a review of your meal when it doesn't qualify?" Chef stared at him. "You write a review based on your experience with the food that has been served to you, and you write it fairly."

Cardenas cocked his head to the side and let a slight smile peak at the corner of his mouth. "Let me ask you a question, Chef". "What do you think qualifies someone to be a chef? Is it classical training? Years of experience? Or them being recognized as so?"

It felt like all of the air had been sucked out of the room and the rest of us had disappeared. We were all waiting for Chef's response, and just as he was about to answer, an abrupt bang broke the silence. "Ouch!" Everyone turned to see Tory slowly peering up from under the table while rubbing his head . "I dropped my napkin. Sorry", he said with embarrassment. Thankfully, it cut the tension and brought everything back to focus. Just then, Dani comes around the corner. "Chef, we've got everything plated for the next dish. Ready for service?". "Not just yet, let's give them a little time before we get it out", he says, breaking his gaze from Cardenas before heading back into the kitchen.

Paola reached for the bottle of cabernet from the center of the table and pours herself another glass. "Here, my love," Miguel said as he attempted to pass the water carafe to her. "Have some more water." "I'm having another glass of wine, but thank you for being so concerned", she fired back at him. "That's going to be your third glass, though. I don't want you to overdo it is all I'm saying". Kamryn and I exchanged glances again, knowing full well what was about to happen. Paola leaned forward and moved the glass of wine closer to her plate. "I am an adult, Miguel", she fired back at him. "You don't have to monitor how much I drink, or remind me of how much I've had. I will drink what I want to and when I want to." Miguel shook his head, but quickly realized that that was a mistake.

"Fine. Okay, you're right, you know when you've had too much", he said with his hand outstretched in surrender. "You're goddamned right, I'm right. You always try to babysit me, and think that you're somehow in charge of what I consume", she said. "I'm tired of it, Miguel". Miguel reached his hand across the table to try and calm Paola with his touch, but she wants no part of it. "Do not touch me!", she laughed. "You always think that touching me softly is going to calm me down, but it is truly so very patronizing and insulting."

Mr. Cardenas was visibly uncomfortable and attempted to change the subject. "Uh, Paola, I can't help but notice your accent. Where is it that you're from", he asked, holding his breath in hopes that she wouldn't take offense. "Thank you very much!", she said. "My family is from Sao Paulo, Brazil but I spent a lot of time traveling with them all over when I was growing up, so I consider myself to be a citizen of the world". She was flattered and delighted by the positive attention that was on her. "That's wonderful. I always tell my students that they should take any opportunity that they can to travel."

"I thought you were a food critic, Mr. Cardenas?", Tory asked with his mouth half full, and once again, awkward tension had taken a seat at the table. "Excuse me," he said. "I meant to refer to them as my former students. Many years ago, I was a chef myself and had several restaurants. During that time I had several culinary students under my wing". Kamryn nudged Tory with her elbow to get his attention. "What kind of food did you serve at your restaurants?", she asked him. "My establishments specialized in classic French cuisine," he said, dabbing at the corners of his mouth with his cloth napkin. "We were known as some of the most prominent restaurants in New York City, with two of them earning Michelin stars", he said, with his eyes glancing over at Chef as he entered from the kitchen with a fresh napkin for Tory. "It's truly an honor to receive such high recognition," Cardenas announced with a proud and arrogant look on his face. "That's interesting that you say that," Kamryn replied, angling her head to the side and pursing her lips as if she were turning his statement over in her mind trying to make sense of it. "You know, the Michelin guide was originally intended to promote tourism in 1900, which was mainly reserved for upper class Europeans so that they could drive more and buy more Michelin brand tires". Miguel and Paola momentarily paused their exchange of sharp gazes to listen to her. 'A group of French guys literally got together and picked out their favorite places to eat, and deemed them to be special just because they liked the food. Michelin still authoritatively judges restaurants just to promote the Michelin brand… which literally just makes RUBBER TIRES," she emphasized. "Doesn't seem very special if you ask me. Tires and food have nothing to do with each other, and the ratings only matter because people believe that they do. But, congratulations!" She flashed a quick smile to Cardenas and went back to her plate. "Dad, can I have some extra hollandaise", she asked as she looked at Chef who was already beaming at her with pride. "Yep, of course you can, boo", he said, heading toward the kitchen. Lucas must have overheard her request and quickly brought a ramekin to her place setting and spooned more of the velvety sauce on the plate.

"Would anyone else like any extra hollandaise?" he asked. Most of us declined as we were nearly finished with our plates. He walked around to Cardenas' and noticed that most of the crab cake had been flaked apart with very few bites taken. "Mr. Cardenas, is everything alright with your dish? Can I offer you anything?". Cardenas adjusted his sweater vest and laid his fork down beside his plate. "No thank you, young man. Everything is just fine". "Sir, forgive me if you've already spoken with the table about this, but I'd love to know where you're from", he asked, trying to mask his excitement and nervousness. "I've read a lot of your reviews and know a lot about your career, but I don't think I've ever come across that". Lucas and Chef spent many Saturday mornings in the kitchen before breakfast prep, reading through Cardenas' latest reviews, and discussing them at length. Over the past two years, Lucas has come to be a fan of his writing style and strong opinions, and has a running list of the restaurants that Cardenas has critiqued that he hopes to visit.

"My family is from Spain, but I grew up going to boarding school in Britain", he said with a slight smile. "That's really cool! So how did you get into culinary?"Lucas asked, shifting his weight a bit in anticipation. "Well I always loved great food, and even as a child I appreciated the flavors and textures of certain dishes. But my mother was a terrible cook!", he said, shaking his head while the rest of us laughed. "Everything she made was either overcooked, or had absolutely no flavor. I mean she couldn't even boil eggs correctly. She would cook the living shit out of them to the point where the yolks were gray and tough. So when I was in secondary school, I chose to focus my studies on culinary. From there, I enrolled into Westminster Kingsway College in London, and started working as a dishwasher at a very prominent restaurant called Wiltons to pay for school". "Wiltons!", Paola loudly exclaimed, her eyes wide with excitement. "You've heard of it all the way over here?" Cardenas asked, genuinely curious. "Of course I have! It's world-renowned", she said to him with a confused look, as if it should never have occurred to him that she wouldn't know about the restaurant. "I spent a lot of time in London when I was a teenager, and my friends and I would go there for the oyster bar and cocktails after fashion shows or a long day of go-sees with different designers". "Well, then. That's quite the coincidence," he said, scrambling to cover up his assumption. "For you, it must be," Paola said with a sarcastic smile. "I beg your pardon?". The statement was quick and sharp like a needle prick. "I wouldn't say that it's a coincidence for me. More like you worked a lower than entry level position at a restaurant that I frequented. So, for you, it must feel like a coincidence". Miguel took a slow deep breath and reached for the bottle of wine, while the rest of us braced for the inevitable impact. "You know, I understand that you attended a British boarding school and had elite culinary training, just as our dear Chef did at the Culinary Institute of Lenotre. But I think that with all of your training and high class experience, and expert criticism, you forget that there are others who have also experienced the finer things in life. Especially if they don't look like you." Once again, the room fell silent and Cardenas was left speechless. Again, he readjusted his sweater vest and cleared his throat to gather his thoughts. "Chef, I don't believe you answered my question. I'm very eager to hear your thoughts on what qualifies someone to be a chef."

"A chef is one who runs the entire operation! Cooking great food isn't good enough. You have to prepare menus, keep up with vendor practices, and put together a team that will keep the kitchen successful. Professional training is definitely important, but I wouldn't disqualify someone who can cook their ass off just because they didn't go to culinary school", Chef said. "You can learn a lot from being in the kitchen, and studying other chefs. Hell, Gordon Ramsay and Tom Colicchio didn't go to culinary schools, and they are well-respected chefs. The world recognizes them as chefs."

"I didn't know they didn't go to culinary school!" Miguel said, "Honey, did you know that?" he asked Paola. "No, I had no idea! They're both so well known that I doubt anyone even bothered to ask." Chef snapped his fingers and pointed at Paola highlighting the accuracy of her statement. "That's exactly my point. When you're great at what you do, no one is going to check for your credentials. I can't remember the last time an employer even asked to see my diploma. Once they saw that I had been an Executive Chef and had real experience, that's all that mattered."

Cardenas took a long slow sip of his wine, and nodded his head. "You make a good argument. I guess things are a bit different for me since I'm a bit old school. The title of chef was originally a coveted and respected title, and it came with a lot of prestige."

"That's definitely carried over in some ways, because now we have celebrity chefs and competition cooking shows that promise money and Executive Chef positions", Lucas said. "I would love to get good enough at cooking to where I can get on one of those shows and have my own place."

"That's a lot of work!" Chef and Cardenas said simultaneously. "Tell him about it, Chef!" Cardenas said, smiling and shaking his head. "Don't get me wrong, I love culinary but it's definitely not an easy job. I mean think about it, you're spending hours in a hot kitchen with sometimes 10 or more other people. It's loud, there's always something going on, you have to manage the front of the house and the kitchen, and God forbid someone on the line calls out and you have to accommodate for that."

"He's right", Cardenas started. "And I don't know what the pay is like here, but in the UK and in the States, most Executive Chefs make roughly $100,000 to maybe $200,000 at a very high end fine dining establishment". "And by the time you make your money," Chef added "you don't have time to be away from the kitchen to even spend it or enjoy much of your life. You're literally always in the kitchen, unless you set yourself up to have scheduled time off."

Lucas lowered his brow in deep thought. "I definitely thought chefs made more money. How come some of the chefs that we see on TV are able to have multiple restaurants and still be on TV", he asked.

"That's just it", Dani intervened. "They have made it to a level of success and notoriety to where they can just attach their name to a restaurant without having to actually be in the kitchen cooking". "You know that Wolfgang Puck has like twenty restaurants. You think he's flying all over the world making appetizers in all those kitchens, dumb ass?" She said as she hit her brother on the back of the head. "I don't know! I never thought about it like that, stupid!", Lucas yelled and hit her back on the arm. Cardenas is visibly shocked and concerned at their behavior, and looks to the rest of us for explanation, but we're all unphased. I've been around Lucas and Dani long enough to understand their sibling dynamic and the delicate balance between them. Dani is a textbook first born daughter. Responsible, a little controlling, independent, and trustworthy, but thinks that her brother's wellbeing is somehow her responsibility. Likely the results of having to care for him during their childhood while their parents worked, even though she's only three years older than him. Lucas is still figuring out where he fits in the world, but also has tunnel vision when it comes to his goals. He wants more than anything to be a chef and open his own restaurant, but also make his sister proud even if he doesn't say it. His intentions are good for the most part, but he can't seem to get his temper under control or shake his magnetism for trouble. It's gotten a lot better since he's started working so closely with Chef, but there have been plenty of times when the two of them have had some intense conversations.

"Please excuse me," Paola said, folding her napkin as she stood to leave the table, stumbling a bit as she walked toward the hallway. Dani and Lucas emerged from the kitchen to clear our plates for the next course. Kamryn and Tory were scraping away at the last bits of sauce on their plate before handing them over. "I take it you both enjoyed your meal?" Cardenas asked the two of them. "Mhm!" Kamryn said, nodding her head with her mouth full. "Yeah, it's definitely one of my favorite things to eat. But I'll never turn down a good steak and mashed potatoes", Tory said. "Classic dish. There's nothing in the world like a perfectly cooked steak," Cardenas said, taking a sip from his glass of wine. "And what about you, Kamryn? What's your favorite dish?", he asked. "I actually really like breakfast food, so pancakes and french toast. But they have to be prepared well. Like the pancakes have to be the perfect balance of fluffy in the middle and crispy on the edges, and I only like french toast that's made with brioche and vanilla bean in the batter." Cardenas was impressed by her taste. "I'm the same way when it comes to food," he said. "Especially those classic staple dishes that I love." "What are some of your favorite foods, Mr. Cardenas?", Miguel asked.

"I love it when people ask this question," Cardenas said. He had an amused smile on his face and folded his cloth napkin into his lap. "I'll give you a couple of hints, but you have to guess, okay?" "It's got a flaky crust, a savory sauce, and it reminds me of home."

"Beef wellington!" Kamryn shouted out first. "Nope!". "Samosas!", Miguel said. "Not quite", Cardenas replied. "Gazpacho!", Tory shouted confidently. We all turned toward him, both perplexed and surprised by his response. "So close!" said Cardenas. "Do you even know what Gazpacho is?" Kamryn laughed. "I don't, I just figured it's something that might have a crust on it," Tory shrugged as we laughed. "Gazpacho is a cold soup, man", Chef said. "And it's delicious," Cardenas added. "But not my favorite. Chicken pot pie is my all-time favorite dish. That fact always surprises people because I think they expect me to like very fancy food, or something rich and difficult to make," he said. "Yeah I would've taken you for a coq au vin kind of guy!", Kamryn said. "Right? That's definitely what I would've thought," Miguel said with a chuckle. "Cocoa what?", Tory asked. Kamryn put her arm around her uncle's shoulder. "I'll tell you about it another time," she said.

"What is it about chicken pot pie that you enjoy?" Miguel asked. "A lot of it has to do with the feelings that I have associated with it. Feelings of comfort, and home. I always say that every good chef remembers the first time they have their favorite dish, and I definitely remember mine," Cardenas said, just as Chef returned from the kitchen to check in on things. "I bet Chef Kababo recalls the first time he had his favorite dish too. I was in secondary school, and was very homesick as I hadn't been back home with my parents in nearly a year. A classmate of mine invited me to have dinner with his family, and his mother brought a perfect chicken pot pie to the table. I just remember that it was unlike anything I had ever had before. The crust was buttery and thick, and the filling was decadent and creamy, seasoned with lots of thyme and spices that really made me feel like I was close to home."

"I know what you mean. Most of my favorite foods are tied to memories that I have like cooking with my grandmother, or from culinary school in Europe. But one of my favorite dishes to make is chicken masala', Chef said. "Ooh, I don't think you've made that in a long time", Kamryn said. "Yeah it's been a while. You know I rarely cook at home!" Cardenas chuckled a bit. "I've noticed that people expect chefs to always be cooking at home or having elaborate dishes for every meal. That isn't the case at all".

"Not at all!", I exclaimed. "I can't tell you how many times I've watched him eat homemade charcuterie or fast food for dinner because he refused to cook!". Chef looked at me and couldn't help but to laugh. "You know I'm right!", I said. "I'll never deny that! After years of being in the kitchen and catering, the last thing I want to do when I get home most days is get back into the kitchen to make something to eat. I'm exhausted!"

"I know that feeling all too well," Cardenas agreed. "People would also be surprised to know that as much as I love well-prepared food, and can do it myself, I also love a good fast food cheeseburger and fries. When I'm not dining at a restaurant that I am reviewing, I can usually be found at home with a greasy bag of take out, and my feet up on the coffee table."

"Yeah, that definitely sounds like Chef ", Miguel added. "This is the first time he's cooked for me and Paola, but he's quick to meet us at a local spot for dinner and drinks."

"Where is Paola anyway?", Chef asked. "She may have gone to the restroom. I'll go check on her", Miguel said as he excused himself from the table.

Cardenas is halfway through his third glass of wine when he spots Dani walking in from the kitchen with a pitcher of water in her hands. "You there, miss!" he says, startling her a bit. "Yes?" "We were just talking about some of our favorite meals and the memories that we have attached to them. Would you care to share yours?"

"Oh, um sure," Dani said as she nervously looked around the room. "I would have to say arroz con leche. My grandmother used to make it for me and Luc when we were little, and it was always such a special treat." "Oh yeah, I remember that!" Lucas added. "She used to toast the rice a little bit and it would make the house smell kind of like popcorn".

"I forgot about that part!" Dani said with a smile. "She would put the arroz con leche in these little yellow bowls, and the three of us would sit at the kitchen table and eat it while we waited for mom or dad to come home from work."

"That's a beautiful memory to have. Do you happen to have the recipe?", Cardenas asked with genuine curiosity. "I don't think she ever wrote any of her recipes down or anything, but I could probably remake it if I tried."

"That would be a beautiful way to honor her and the memories you shared", Cardenas added.

"I think you're right, I'll have to do that someday," Dani said softly. She was surprised by his kindness. Up to this point, everything that she had heard about the infamous Antonio Cardenas emphasized how sharp and uncompromising he was. But this conversation showed her that there might be more to the critic than his reputation would have her believe.

"I've noticed that many people have memories of their favorite food that are tied to someone in their lives that they love dearly. I think that's beautiful," Cardenas said. "It is beautiful," I added. "I have an auntie who makes a huge pot of gumbo for our whole family on New Year's Day. Just like Chef said that he looked forward to Christmas morning for his dad's eggs benedict, I would go to sleep on New Year's Eve ecstatic about the meal I'd have at my grandmother's house the next day."
"Gumbo? I don't think I've ever had that before. What is it?," Lucas asked. "It's so good! The best way that I can describe it is a rich and savory stew with shrimp and crabmeat, sausage and vegetables, and it's served over rice. But that doesn't even do it justice. She would only make it once a year because it was expensive to buy all of the ingredients to feed our extended family, but I think that's what made it so special."

"That's awesome," Chef said. "Food is such an expression and labor of love. From preparing it, to serving it to others, and watching them enjoy it. In a way, it's an extension of the cook. They put their energy and time into creating something from raw ingredients, with the intention of it being tasty and nourishing for whoever would be eating it. Where there's food there's community. It's where decisions are made, where discussions are had, and where we ultimately make memories without us even knowing it. Food is one thing that every culture and group of people have in common. We can look back at ancient civilizations and see written evidence of families coming together to share meals with their utensils and bowls. It's an intimate thing to cook for people and break bread with them, and knowing that it's something that they look forward to and enjoy makes it that much better."

"Would you say that that's why some chefs don't like it when guests ask for substitutions?" Lucas asked him. "Absolutely!" Chef replied enthusiastically. "I cannot stand it when I prepare a dish and it is described in the menu, and a customer asks for a key ingredient to be substituted for something that completely alters what I intended"

"I can agree with you there. The only time that I can justify making a substitution at a good restaurant is if the person has a food allergy; and even then I feel like they should order something that doesn't have their allergens in it. Outside of that, there is no excuse," Cardenas insisted.

Just then, we heard Paola and Miguel in a bit of a heated exchange in the next room. "What is your problem?" Paola said sharply. We all stopped and looked around at each other with concern, but Chef was unphased. None of this was new to him, and was already mentally prepared for another argument between the couple before the end of the night. "What don't you understand? This is why I ask you not to drink so much when we're out! Look at you!" Miguel snapped at her. "I told you, I'm fine!" Paola said with a sarcastic happy tone. We heard them tussle a bit and then came silence. Then intermittent rhythmic beats and the sound of Paola's jewelry clanging together in unison. I grimaced and looked over at Chef who was shaking his head back at me. We all knew exactly what was going on, but none of it was atypical behavior for those two. Cardenas was stunned but did his best to conceal his secondhand embarrassment. This went on for what felt like the longest five minutes, until Paola gasped as we heard the crash and shattering of something hitting the floor.

Crab-Cake Benedict

Ingredients

Jumbo Lump Crab - 227 g (8 oz)

Panko Bread Crumbs - 84 g

Onion - 15 g (½ oz)

Bell Pepper - 15 g (½ oz)

Celery - 15 g (½ oz)

Garlic - 15 g (½ oz)

Butter - 56 g

Cajun Seasoning (no salt added) - 28 g (2 tbsp)

Smoked Paprika - 14 g (1 tbsp)

Coarse Black Pepper - 14 g (0.5 tbsp)

Coarse Kosher Salt - 14 g (1 tbsp)

Whole Grain Mustard - 28 g (2 tbsp)

Mayonnaise - 14 g (1 tbsp)

English Muffin - 1 ea

Egg Whites - 2 ea

Egg Yolks - 6

Water - 14 ml (1 tbsp)

Cayenne Pepper - 7 g (¼ tbsp)

Coarse Kosher Salt - 7 g (½ tbsp)

Lemon - 1/2 each

Louisiana Hot Sauce (Or your local favorite brand Hot Sauce) 14 ml (1 tbsp)

Worcestershire Sauce - 14 ml (1 tbsp)

Unsalted Butter - 454 g (1 pound)

Water - ½ fill

White Vinegar - 14 ml (1 tbsp)

Eggs - 2 per 8 oz of crab

Tools

Whisk
Fish Spatula
Rubber Spatula
Medium Metal Mixing Bowl
Medium Saute Pan
Small Sauce Pot
Sheet Pan

The traditional Eggs Benedict was my favorite dish when I was a child. My father would only cook it on or around the holidays but I couldn't wait! It was the sauce that did it for me, it was rich and flavorful and the whole combination was just bomb.

Crab-Cake Mix

First let's prepare our aromatics! Onion, Bellpepper, Garlic, & Celery are to be small diced and placed into a medium mixing bowl. It's important to small dice the aromatics because they will be presented in the dish and you would not want to eat large chunks of onion in your Crab-Cake. (Onion, Bell Pepper, Celery, & Garlic). With a medium saute pan and your flame on medium-high allowing your pan to fully come up to temperature before adding 14 g (1 tbsp) of butter to the pan. In with the aromatics, Coarse Kosher Salt, Coarse Black Pepper, Cajun Seasoning , & Smoked Paprika. Give the pan a couple of tosses to fully incorporate the spices and to prevent burning. Once the onions turn translucent you are finished cooking, this should take about 5 mins or so. Your point is to remove the water from your aromatics and incorporate flavor. Set into a medium mixing bowl to which we will add the other ingredients to.

In that same mixing bowl add the Panko Bread Crumbs, Whole Grain Mustard, Mayonnaise, Eggs Whites (2), Jumbo Lump Crab, additional Coarse Kosher Salt 14 g

(1 tbsp), & Coarse Black Pepper 7g (½ tbsp) and with a rubber spatula mix all of the ingredients together gently. Your objective is NOT to break all of the Jumbo Lump Crab up into smaller pieces, some of them will break of course and that's fine but you want to preserve a lot of it. Once everything is mixed together, set in the refrigerator for 20-30 mins so the mix can cool off which will allow you to form the Crab-Cake shape better.

Once the Crab-Cake mix is cooled take 57 g (2 oz) and form a hockey puck shape and place them onto a sheet pan. You are looking for 76 mm (3 inches) in diameter and 25 mm (1 inch) thick.

Hollandaise Sauce

Egg Yolks - 12 (Keep the egg whites for the Crag Cake)
Water - 14 ml (1 tbsp)
Cayenne Pepper - (7 g ¼ tbsp)
Coarse Kosher Salt - (14 g ½ tbsp)
Lemon - 1/2 each
Louisiana Hot Sauce (Or your local favorite brand Hot Sauce) 14 ml (1 tbsp)
Worcestershire Sauce - 14 ml (1 tbsp)
Unsalted Butter - 454 g (1 pound)

Tools

Small to Medium Sauce Pot x 2
Metal Medium Mixing Bowl
Whisk
Towel

You can execute this 1 of 2 ways, the traditional path which is more labor intensive but it keeps you grounded to the experience or you can use a blender. I'm going to teach you the traditional way however if you want to exchange your wisk for the blender blade please feel free.

This sauce is touchy and if you are not careful it will break and you will need to restart the process. We will make a bain marie to help keep the temperature limited. With a small sauce pot filled with ½ water you want to bring this to a soft boil. In a separate Sauce Pot melt the 454 g of butter and set it close to the Bain Marie beauce you will add the melted butter to the mixing bowl when it's time.

Place the 12 Egg Yolks into a metal mixing bowl and add your 14 ml of water, then place the bowl on top of the small sauce pot with boiling water making it a bain marie. With a whisk you will continuously stir the eggs in a circular motion mildly to prevent the Egg Yolks from turning into scrambled eggs and allowing the temperature to slowly rise. You will know when your egg yolks become more fluid and a slight change in color with small bubbles along the edges that it's time to add the melted butter.

Once the egg yolks are up to temperature slowly add the melted butter (slow drizzle) into the mixing bowl while continuously mixing the entire time. If you stop mixing the likelihood of breaking the sauce or making scrambled eggs increases. So when making this sauce there are two things that are important:

1. The slow drizzle of the melted butter into the egg yolks, because pouring the butter too fast will break the sauce.

2. Continuously mix with the whisk in the metal mixing bowl in a circular fashion in an aggressive fashion until the sauce is complete. This aggressive mixing motion is what the blender does when choosing to take that path.

Ultimately you will use one hand to pour the melted butter in a slow drizzle into the egg yolks and with the other hand continuously whisk in a circular motion aggressively to emulsify the two liquids.

Once you have added all of the butter you can remove the bowl from the sauce pot and add the remaining ingredients. Your sauce is complete, set it aside to use a bit later.

English Muffin

If you can find a dope baker that does these, fresh english muffins are mad bomb. However the store bought ones will work just fine. Slice them in half horizontally and toast them with butter in a saute pan. Place them onto the canvas (also known as a plate).

Back to the Crab-Cake Mix

Using a medium Saute Pan with the flame set to medium-high, add 14 g (1 tbsp) of butter once the pan is up to temperature. I can normally fit 4 in a pan at a time, but I would suggest that you comfortably fit as many as you can depending on the size of your pan. You are going to Saute them evenly on both sides to give some caramelization and crisp to the edges. If you are using a Saute Pan that can go into the oven safely do so after 3 (ish) mins of sauteing each side. Remember this isn't a science, but an artform. If you notice your Crab-Cakes are not caramelized and crispy, cook them a bit longer to achieve that texture. If you are not willing to place your pan into the oven just turn your flame down to a simmer and allow them to cook evenly on each side. I would prefer you not to flip them more than once, because I've noticed that the more you touch them the more likely it is that the Crab-Cakes will break apart. Ideally, you'll want to flip them once, place them into the oven for 10 mins at 350 degrees and onto your canvas (also known as a plate) once fully cooked. You will place 1 Crab-Cake on top of each halved English Muffin.

Poaching the Eggs

Water - ½ fill
White Vinegar - 14 ml (1 tbsp)
Eggs - 2 per order

Using the same bain marie pot water, refill ½ way with water & add 14 ml (1 tbsp) of White Vinegar while bringing it back to a medium boil. Crack 1 egg at a time and place it into the medium boiling water. The reason you want a medium boil is so the bubbles agitate the egg and massage it into place without you doing anything else. You can add multiple eggs just as long as you do it one by one. You will only poach these eggs for 3-4 mins each, we don't want hard boiled eggs. The center should be creamy and runny while the egg whites are fully cooked.

Garnish

Green Onions or Chives

Once finished place 1 egg each on top of the Crab-Cake. Now you are going to sauce your dish, I would normally use a 2 oz ladle however you can use a tablespoon or a larger serving spoon depending on what's available for you. I love the sauce so I would use 2 ladles or (4 oz) of the lovely ingredient. Take some fresh Green Onions or Chives and thinly slice them on an extreme bias (dionangally) for a great garnish .

Canvas (Also Known as a plate) > Toasted English Muffin > Pan Seared Crab-Cake Mix > Poached Egg > Hollandaise Sauce > Thinly Sliced Chives or Green Onions

Chapter 10

Sex and the Village

There is a common notion that out of all the millions of sperm your father produced, YOU fought your way through and survived to fertilize your mothers egg. A lot of people relate this survival and fighting to some random act of Nature, God, or Self. However, my perspective is quite different. Out of the, let's say 3 million sperm my father produced, we were not in contest whatsoever. I had 2,999,999 escorts ensuring my safe passage to my predestined egg. That single egg had my name on it thousands of years ago and no other soul was ever in position to claim it but me. I also relate this to life and the illusion of "not enough" when there is actually an overwhelming abundance. When you know there is an abundance, there is no need to fight, struggle or even survive. The only thing to do is live and experience.

– Kababo

Chef rushed toward the hallway and the rest of us followed behind him, to find Miguel and Paola completely disheveled. They stood there, adjusting their clothing as they looked at the pile of broken black plaster beneath their feet. Paola was relatively unphased as she tinkered with the gold charm bracelet dangling from her left wrist, reattaching the clasp that had come undone. She pulled her long wavy hair up into a ponytail, and looked at the group of us with a smile as if nothing had happened. A much more apologetic Miguel kneeled down to try and gather the broken pieces, muttering an "I'm so sorry, Chef" without meeting Chef's gaze. "It was an accident," he said. "Let me know how much it was, and I'll be happy to replace it for you, bro". Chef kneeled beside him and scooped up the rest of the pieces into his hands. "It's only one of it's kind and holds more sentimental value to me than anything else. It's okay, though. We can glue it back together." Miguel was heartbroken and slightly embarrassed at the thought of disappointing his friend. "What was it, Chef?" Lucas asked. "Yeah I noticed it when you were giving us the tour, but didn't ask what it was", said Dani. "It's a black buddha statue that was given to me by one of my mentors, Pastor Rudy Rasmus. It's not your typical buddha though, this one has a beard in three braids."

The marble hallway counter is scattered with relics and keepsakes from Chef's childhood and early in his career. A lot of them are gifts from culinary mentors and souvenirs that he's picked up along his travels overseas when he was in school.

"Pastor Rudy was a major influence in my life at a very pivotal time. He's the best example of a Christian that I've ever encountered. When you think of a black Christian pastor, you might think of a big guy with some flashy jewelry who is always talking about the Bible. Maybe self-righteous and arrogant. Pastor Rudy is everything but that. I never felt judged by him, or like I had to put on heirs and be a super cleaned up presentable version of myself. He's the kind of guy that truly has a heart for people and meets them exactly where they are in life. When I was a kid, any time I questioned an elder about the Bible or Christianity, I was chastised or told that I was being disrespectful or that I didn't have enough faith. Pastor Rudy never made me feel that way. Outside of my family, he's one of the only people that wasn't afraid to call me out on my bullshit and love me through it. When I was engaged to my ex-wife, he was the only person that was honest with me, and told me not to marry her. He saw the toxicity in our relationship, and told me that it would never change.

"Damn. That had to hurt," Miguel said as he leaned back again against the counter and crossed his arms in front of him. "I saw it coming, I knew the relationship was toxic. I mean, not even my family members said anything to me like that. Their responses to us were sort of like "Oh wow, okay. Well, if that's what you want, then we're happy for you." You know, your family is going to support your decisions when they see how passionate you are about them. And at the end of the day, they just want to see you happy so I don't fault my family at all. But Pastor Rudy did what my family likely felt that they couldn't. He refused to officiate our wedding. And as disappointed as I was, I completely respected the fact that he stuck to his convictions and didn't commit to something that he didn't agree with. He truly saw me for who I was as a person, and planted seeds in me that are still producing fruit. He was a huge proponent for therapy and inner healing, and connected me with my first therapist."

"What was therapy like for you?" Tory asked. "I've always wanted to go just to talk about some things, but I'm not sure what to expect."

"It was one of the best things I could have ever done for myself. Therapy helps you to learn things about yourself in ways that you otherwise wouldn't have. It's like you're able to sit down with this person who is completely objective, and they can help to open up your mind and help you to spread out all of the pieces that make up who you are," he said with some of the broken statue in his hands. "They help you to see where things need more attention, and what areas have created cycles and behaviors that you may not have noticed. It can be scary, and uncomfortable at times because you're being asked to address things that you've never known about yourself. But it's such a crucial

component to knowing who you are as a person, and to move forward as the healthiest

version of yourself. You get as much out of it as you intend to. If you go into it wanting to

work on yourself, then that's exactly what will come of it."

Tory fiddled with a tiny replica of the Eiffel Tower that he picked up from the

countertop as he was absorbing his brother's words. "You don't hear of a lot of Black

people or people of color talking about emotional healing and wellness," Tory added.

"That's really cool that your pastor was such an advocate for that, and encouraged you

to go."

"Yeah, for sure. Pastor Rudy is one of a kind. He would intentionally lie to me

sometimes just to highlight how naive and gullible I was! Telling me tiny lies about

frivolous things and major events, I would believe every word until I finally figured out

his motive. He wasn't the type to just give me a pat on the back, but more like a swift

kick in the ass! That kind of love helped me to see that I shouldn't be so easily led on by

others, and that I had to question and investigate things for myself. A lot of times, you'll

hear people talk about how their religious leaders might talk down to them because of

their position of power. But Pastor Rudy was never like that. He never talked to me like I

was beneath him, or like his life was somehow more acceptable to God than mine.

What made me trust him as a leader was his honesty and full transparency about his life

as a pimp years before he became a pastor. We would talk about the lessons that he

learned through his experiences and how he ended up in that lifestyle, but I appreciated that it never felt like his past was too far removed from his life as a pastor. Our conversations were always relatable, and eye opening for me. He taught me that people watch how I maneuver through life, and how some don't like it so they'll be sure to do whatever they can to keep me from the goals that I've set out. And so far, he's been correct. I've had to cut off a lot of people in my life because of the way they viewed me, and how jealousy was a driving force for them to work with me. I've had people literally sabotage my work because they were jealous of me."

"Wait what?" Tory said in disbelief as he helped to pick up plaster pieces from the floor and hold them in his shirt.

"Yep. This guy had been working for me at one of my restaurants for a few months, and in passing he would make jokes that always seemed to have some truth to them. I asked him to be my sous chef when I started working as a private chef for the Defensive End of the Houston Texans Jadeveon Clowney to prepare meal preps for him during the off season. I asked my sous chef to prepare five different vegetables and three proteins across five meals. Instead of doing what I asked, he deliberately fucked it up and made only one vegetable and cooked it with no seasoning. He wanted me to give my client something that he didn't ask for, and made me look like I couldn't adequately do my job. When I asked him to correct it, he straight up said "No. I don't want you to win". I fired him on the spot and made him leave the kitchen. I was stunned and it took a minute for me to actually process what this dude had done. But I couldn't be upset about it because he had told me from the beginning through his jokes that he was jealous of me. Some people are on this Earth just to hate. That's their goal and sole purpose, and it's up to us to recognize them when we see them and move accordingly. That's what Pastor Rudy was trying to teach me all those years ago. So when I walk through the house and see this bearded buddha statue, it reminds me to keep my eyes open and be mindful of the company that I keep."

Chef gathered the rest of the broken buddha pieces into a small woven basket and set it aside. He patted Miguel on the shoulder to let him know that all was well and forgiven. Dani had wandered down the hallway a bit, carefully tracing her fingertips along the cabinet top until she reached the large gold trimmed white plate with the French flag painted on it, perched on it's own ledge. "Chef, where did you get this plate?"

Chef walked over to it and smiled with pride and nostalgia. "This is really cool. Years ago I was working at Drexelhouse with one of my culinary mentors, Chef Philippe. He's your typical pretentious asshole French chef, and he believed that his opinion on food is the end all be all. If you think of the hard ass caricature that Gordon Ramsay plays into on TV, that's Chef Philippe. Aside from his attitude, what made him stand out was his skills in the kitchen. He taught me the importance of taking my time in the kitchen, and how to visualize the way I want the food to look before actually cooking it. He would always give me shit about the way that I cooked, but it was because he liked me and wanted me to live up to my culinary potential. And if I fucked up, he would yell at me and reprimand me in ways that he wouldn't do for others when they made the same mistakes. He saw what I was capable of and held me to that standard at all times, so I had no choice but to be great in the kitchen. He also indirectly taught me that I shouldn't be an asshole to people. The way he treated my peers was definitely harsh, so I learned that if you want people to thrive in anything that they're doing, you have to be kind and patient with them. Especially in high-stress environments like we were working in.

Everyone knew that we were in the presence of greatness when we got the opportunity to watch him cook. He had the opportunity to host a special dinner for Master Chefs from all over the world, and I volunteered to help. It was a multi-course meal, and Chef Philippe asked me to plate a really tasty ceviche at my station. The fact that he allowed me to help meant that he trusted and respected my abilities, so that was very special to me at that time in my career. It was an honor to be in the room with those chefs who were recognized as being true Master Chefs. This plate here is a Master Chef ceremonial plate that Chef Philippe gave me to commemorate the occasion. I'll never forget that experience. Probably one of the coolest things I've done in my career."

"This whole area is sort of the Hall of Fame for the mentors and teachers in my life. I believe it's important to honor the people in your life that have helped you move forward in your journey. Each of these items here has a story or a life lesson attached to it, and I keep them here to remind me of those lessons."

"There are a few things here that I collected during my time over in France," he said as he pointed at the section of keepsakes. Tory picked up a small glass vial etched with flakes of gold and filled with a thousand tiny deep red threads. "Are these pieces of flower petals?"

"Close! It's a spice called saffron, and it comes from the inside of a beautiful purple flower that's grown in Iran. It's one of the most expensive spices in the world because of how special the flower is. This is only a few ounces, but it's rather expensive."

"Where did you get it from," Lucas asked as he and Tory marveled at the spice as if it were treasure. "A culinary mentor and dear friend of mine, Chef Kiran Verma gave that to me. She's the chef and owner of a fine dining Indian restaurant in Houston, and she's easily the most hardworking person I've ever worked for. She's been in the restaurant game for over 30 years, and has an immaculate palette. As talented and driven as she is, she's always remained humble and treated me and others with dignity and respect. When I started working for Chef Kiran, I didn't know anything about working with Indian food, and I was pretty ignorant to everything that was going on. She was really patient with me though, and taught me about fine dining in a way that I had never experienced before. We did a lot of event catering, and the restaurant offered an elaborate high tea on Saturdays with a special menu that patrons had to request with 24 hours notice. I learned a lot about different foods that I hadn't ever had before, and the operational facets of a busy top-tier restaurant. I was only able to work with her for a few short months, but every day was impactful and I still use a lot of the lessons that I got from that time. She really believed in my talents, and she trusted me to support her and her staff when it got hectic."

Next to Chef Kiran's gift sits a brown leather satchel with straps wrapped and tied around it. "I know what this one is!" Kamryn said to her dad. "Yep, that one's really special. That's the knife that Chef Matthew Lynn gave to me when I graduated from Culinary Institute Lenotre. He's the first instructor that I had who recognized that I would make a strong leader. He caught on to how I would finish my work in the kitchen first and then would help others so that we could stay on time, and told me that that type of management would help me to run a kitchen well. This dude is a true Texas redneck by the looks of him. He was raised around the bigotry and racism that's commonplace in the South, and yet he's the most kind and loving person with no tolerance for racism. He was very honest with me about my cooking skills, and even complimented me at times but he noticed my arrogance right away. He's such an inspiration to me. Before I knew I wanted to move here to Costa Rica, Chef Matthew would tell me stories about his travels all over the world and how he spent a few years cooking here and how much he loved the people and the culture."

"When did he give you this knife?" Lucas asked as he carefully picked up the wrapped blade, but stopped short as he realized he hadn't asked permission. Chef, already looking at him, smiled and nodded in approval. He untied the worn leather straps and unfolded the satchel, revealing a warped eight inch knife with a smooth black handle. "Why is it all bent out of shape like this? Did you drop it or something?" he asked.

"Right before I graduated, the school presented me with it as a gift. And I guess I thought I was hot shit after they gave it to me, because Chef Matthew took it from me and started hammering the back of the blade with a mallet. As if it didn't mean anything to me at all."

"Why would he do that?"Lucas asked with his face scrunched in confusion. "He told me that I was talented and great at what I do, and that he was certain that I would be recognized many times for my talent throughout my career, but that I should never let the accolades get to me and that I should never forget to be humble. I never forgot that lesson, and never got rid of that knife."

Hanging on the wall just above Chef's collection of treasures, is a framed map of Vendee, France with a signature scribbled on the lower left corner. Tucked into the edges of the frame is a small menu with the words "Le Balata" printed at the top.

"These last two here are from my time in Vendee, France. I worked with Chef Nicholas Boucher at Le Balata, and with Chef David Boumaud at Le Petit St. Thomas. Both of these guys are some of the most badass chefs in the world. Chef David is the first chef that I worked with in France, and I've never met anyone that moves as fast as he does. He does everything fast. He gets out of the car fast, moves in the kitchen fast, goes to the restroom fast, and always operates at the highest level of perfection - and his crew knew to keep up with him no matter the cost. I didn't understand how someone could move that quickly and not make mistakes, but after watching him and getting to know him on a personal and professional level, I learned that it all came with practice and that he did make mistakes - they were just corrected as quickly as he made them. It was from working closely with him that I learned that maintaining a Michelin Guide level restaurant required nonstop work and attention and that the Executive Chef had to make sure that that work happened every single day. I realized much later that I don't want that work to happen nonstop, because of the toll it took on my body and the overall wellbeing of myself and my team. "

Paola returned from the dining table with a glass of wine in her hand and joined us in the hallway. "Vendee!" she squealed as she pointed at the frame. "That's one of my favorite cities to visit in France! Did you stay there long, Chef K?" Chef smiled at her and looked over at Miguel who was blushing with slight embarrassment. "Only for a few months, but I really enjoyed it. Chef David invited me to stay with him and his lovely wife and their two sons while I was there, and they really took care of me. They were extremely loving and kind to me, and welcomed me into their home and their family as if I were a blood relative."

"I remember having lovely meals in Vendee when I visited, and it was always with multiple courses. So different from a lot of other cities", Paola added.

"Yeah, that's the way that most restaurants serve food in that area. If you were to go anywhere for lunch or dinner, you would have three to five courses. Le Petit St. Thomas is a Michelin Guide restaurant and spent three years on the list, so Chef David made sure that everything that we served and the way the kitchen ran lived up to that prestige. As high-class as the restaurant was, it was the first one that I had worked at that didn't have a dishwasher. " "What did Chef David have you working on when you were in his kitchen?", Tory asked. "I worked in the starters, so I did a lot of fabrications of lobster and seafood. Chef took a really classic and clean approach to food, and everything was very crisp and precise. So I was able to work with fresh ingredients and prepare them in a way that was very pure. Chef David and I would go to the markets on Fridays and to visit with farmers and bakers around town that he would buy from. That's where I learned about establishing and maintaining relationships with the people that grow and supply the ingredients that I cook with. Every chef should know where their ingredients are from, so that they can trust that they're serving the highest quality food." "That's why you started to grow your garden out there, right Chef?" Lucas asked. "Yeah, that's definitely part of it. There's a lot of gratification that comes from seeing and harvesting the fruit that was once a seedling that you planted. But it's the process between seed and harvest that teaches us to stay in the present and accept what is happening right in front of us. We don't eat the fruit the same day that we plant the seed. It takes time, nutrients, darkness, and a lot of patience. If you can get focused and still enough within yourself to appreciate what is without rushing the process, there comes a deeper appreciation and enjoyment when it's time to have the harvest. That's what brings me the most joy. The process and the appreciation that I feel knowing that everything that I am preparing and feeding to my guests and my family came from

seeds that I hand selected is incomparable. It brings me joy to walk in the garden and

see mounds of dirt that indicate that a new seed has recently been planted. Even

though it hasn't taken root yet, I trust that it will when the time is right. And when that

seed begins to sprout and I can see tiny green leaves emerging from those mounds, I

know that the cycle is moving forward. It means a lot to me.

"It sounds like you've had some really great mentors to guide you through life

and your career, Chef" Dani said. "Absolutely. I truly appreciate each of them for

tolerating my intense arrogance at a time when my insecurities were just as loud as my

talents. Those mentors made a conscious choice to look past that arrogance and teach

me in spite of it. Some people are immediately turned off by arrogance, and it's

understandable. Arrogance can be abrasive and off-putting to some, but to be in this

profession arrogance is sort of a prerequisite. I'll always be grateful that they saw

through it all, and chose to invest their time and resources into me."

Chef gently glided his long fingertips along the edge of the smooth countertop

near his treasures, almost as if to give thanks. We followed him back down the hallway

with our footsteps echoing behind us. Dani and Lucas scurried into the kitchen to

prepare to serve dessert, and we could hear them bickering about something or other

from our seats.

     "What's for dessert?" Tory asked the table. No sooner did we hear the sound of flames igniting from Chef's butane torch. "Creme brulee!", Kamryn squealed with delight.

Chapter 11

Crème Brûlée

The fascination that Americans have with sports amazes me! The time, money, and energy spent on teams fighting for possession of game balls is incredible, and it seems to me that those resources could be better spent on other more important matters. In the community that I grew up in, I was labeled as part of "The African American" group, where the pathways out of poverty were few and often had a ball associated with the journey. That or some hard fought music career that would take you down and through areas of life that you couldn't make it back from. Now, I see so many avenues to wealth other than sports or entertainment. I would have started my culinary career in high school if there was an option to do so, but back in the 90s, Home-Economics was only for girls and they didn't teach many culinary skills. In France, I learned that many programs like Culinary Arts were made available to students as early as the 9th grade, and it was a legitimately skilled craft that they learned rather than a one semester elective. I landed in France during my apprenticeship at the age of 30, and found myself working side by side with 18 year olds. Feeling inadequate because they were so ahead of me in terms of their skillset. I had just completed and paid for a two-year Associates program and they just graduated high school.
– Kababo

"What is that?", Tory said with a confused look on his face. "You've never had crème brûlée?" Miguel and Paola said, surprised and slightly turned on by the fact that they responded in unison.

"Nah! I don't even know what it is. What's in it?" Tory asked. "It's like.." Kamryn started to explain. "Well, it's sort of like a pudding, but not really. Have you had custard before?" she asked. "What the hell is a custard? Isn't that like ice cream?" Tory asked, even more confused than he was before. "It's a French dessert that literally translates as 'burned cream', Cardenas sharply interjected. "It's basically a smooth mixture of egg yolks, heavy cream and sugar, and the sugar on top is caramelized and hardened to create a crispy layer."

"Oh. Yeah I've seen it on menus when I've gone on dates and stuff, but I never ordered it since I didn't know what it was or how to pronounce it," Tory admitted. "And you didn't think to read through the description on the menu?" Cardenas asked him.

Paola cleared her throat and leaned toward Cardenas from across the table. "I believe he just said that he had seen it on menus before, but had never ordered it. So there was no need for you to make that snarky comment." Cardenas was surprised by Paola's assertiveness. "My apologies," he said. " I was only trying to point out that.." "You were trying to point out his ignorance!" Paola interrupted. "And quite frankly, I don't appreciate it. I don't think he appreciates it either." Tory and I exchanged glances, and I nodded in effort to reassure him that everything was okay. "Again," Cardenas said, looking up from his place setting. "My apologies".

Dani and Lucas entered from the kitchen, holding plates with ramekins balanced on top of them. Chef followed closely behind and watched as they both served each of us with our own golden brown dish of his famous crème brûlée.

"This is my all-time favorite dessert," he proudly announced to the table. "It's my favorite thing to order at a restaurant, and one of my favorite things to prepare. I love everything about the process. How you can take simple ingredients like cream, sugar, vanilla bean, and egg yolks and turn it into this rich, decadent custard. It's a fairly simple recipe on paper, but it's really easy to fuck up if you're not careful. So when you get it right, and it tastes the way it's supposed to, that's something to be proud of."

Miguel picked up his dessert spoon and gently broke through the thick, brittle sugar surface in the ramekin, scooping up some of the sweet custard underneath. He brought the spoon to his lips and closed his eyes as he took a bite, shaking his head as he let the richness dissolve in his mouth. "Chef, this is amazing. This is just the first bite, and I'm already thinking about asking for seconds" he said. Chef smiled his big smile, and nodded at him in gratitude. "I'm glad you enjoy it! It's the first dessert that I learned to make in culinary school, and the only dessert that I'm good at."

"Really?" Tory asked him with his mouth full. "Didn't they teach you how to make pastries and all that too?"

"Yeah they did, but that's the one thing I sucked at," Chef said as he laughed at himself. "For whatever reason, I couldn't get the ratios right with wet and dry ingredients, and my pastries would always come out undercooked or overdone. Baking is really a science. Each of the measurements have to be precise in order for the final result to be perfect. And mine never passed the test"

"That's interesting," Cardenas said, looking up from his cell phone that had been holding his attention since dessert was served. "I also found that desserts and pastries were difficult, but I struggled the most in sauces, for some reason. I couldn't get the consistencies right, and would usually burn them right before it was time to present. It took me a long time to master it, but once I did I was able to experiment on my own, and create flavors and textures that were different from what my instructors were teaching."

"I can definitely relate to that," Kababo said. "When a cook is just starting out, everything has to be precise and exactly the way that we're taught. And if they're working under another chef in the kitchen, every plate has to be prepared and presented according to their vision, with no deviation from the script. There's no room to play or experiment with food, and if you're working for an Executive Chef who happens to be a hard ass or they're really dedicated to traditional dishes being prepared the same way each time, you're damn sure not going to have any space for creativity." Cardenas raised his glass in agreement, and I shot an amused glance at Chef noting their common ground.

"So how did you come to find your identity with your own style of food?" Paola asked, winking at Miguel as he spooned some of his crème brûlée into her mouth. "Once I started working for chefs who trusted me with their menus, I was able to expand some of the flavor profiles and give a fresh take to some traditional dishes. But a lot of the confidence that I had about my culinary style came with age and skill. Being comfortable in my own skin and confident in my abilities helped to solidify the fact that I belonged in the kitchen. When you're young, it's easy to get caught up in the demands and pressures of who you think you're supposed to be. You've grown up with your parents and teachers, and even society projecting this acceptable version of who they think you're supposed to be. And you trust them and the constructs that you're born into, because that's the way things have always been for them. So, naturally you want to appease those people in your life that you love and trust, and you might even try to conform to those molds. Until you realize that's not at all who you are, or what you truly want for your life."

"Yes!" Lucas loudly exclaimed, shocking himself by the volume of his voice. "Sorry," he said, with a nervous laugh. "It's just that I relate so much to that sentiment. Like I was saying earlier, my family wants me to go the traditional route of going to college and graduating to become something prestigious like a doctor or lawyer. But that's just not who I am. I love cooking, and really want to make it my career."

Chef could see the drive behind Lucas' eyes, and remembered feeling the same way. "Listen, I'm a rebel. I've always been that way. When people tell me to do something, or say 'Chef, this is what you have to do next', my natural instinct is to buck against it. Because fuck you! I'm me, and I'm going to do whatever I want to do, and I don't care if that goes against what society says I have to do next or if that's what my family says I should do. And I've found that it's in those situations that I'm able to really learn more about myself, push past what I'm expected to do, and trust my own instincts. When I was given an opportunity to be creative and experiment with different ingredients in the kitchen, I was able to come up with some amazing dishes and they impressed the chefs that I worked with. So my advice is to be unafraid to blaze your own trail, and expect resistance from those who have never done what you're trying to do. Understand that fear is the default setting for people who haven't truly pursued their own passions, so they could never tell you what's truly best for you. Only you can know that, and that comes with trusting yourself and being okay with bumping your head a bit along the way. The more you know who you are, the better you are at expressing yourself in every way possible."

"I couldn't agree more," Cardenas said without looking up from his phone.

"Chef, I really like what you said about rebelling against what society deems acceptable, and going against the grain," Paola said as she leaned forward, gathering her long, flowing locks to one shoulder, revealing a bright purple hickey on her neck, before letting it all fall again. "I also consider myself a rebel, and I like to do things that aren't the norm for most people. Take sex, for example." Cardenas choked on his water in shock at Paola's words. He quickly grabbed his cloth napkin, and covered his mouth as he tried to politely excuse himself.

"See!" Paola said with a chuckle. "For some reason, people are so shocked and uncomfortable with the topic of sex, and I've never understood why. It's the most natural thing for our bodies to do, and yet we are told that we cannot discuss it. Or that if we do discuss it, it's somehow inappropriate"

"You'll have to excuse me," Cardenas said as he took another sip of water to collect himself. "It's just that the topic caught me off guard. I'm not used to discussing such personal matters in mixed company, and frankly I thought the conversation that we had earlier would have been sufficient. But, it appears that I am mistaken." Paola squinted a bit at Cardenas, as if to try and read his mind, which must have made him uncomfortable because he shifted his weight in his seat to avoid her gaze.

"What's going through your mind, Mr. Cardenas?", Paola asked, tracing her finger along the rim of her wine glass. "I beg your pardon?" "I asked what was going through your mind, because you seem to be triggered. Sex isn't anything to be ashamed of, you know. It's perfectly normal, and part of a healthy lifestyle if it's done safely and consensually. Don't you agree?"

"I wouldn't say that I'm triggered so much as I am uncomfortable. It's probably due to the way that I was raised. My parents didn't talk about sex, and left it up to my schooling to teach me about sex and reproduction."

"Ah, yes. But did they teach you about pleasure? Or the physical benefits of a healthy sex life?" she asked.

"Now that I think about it, they didn't. They really just focused on the reproductive purpose and the dangers of sexually transmitted diseases and infections."

"That's what I'm saying! Schools perpetuate the idea that sex is shameful and dirty and yet, solely for making babies when there's so much more to it."

"Yeah, my health class showed us a bunch of gross photos that basically made my friends and I want to be nuns forever," Kamryn said with a disgusted grimace on her face. We all laughed at her innocence. "They did the same thing to me when I was in high school, and I remember feeling the exact same way as you. Then I got a girlfriend, and all that went out the window!" Tory said, cracking up with infectious laughter causing the rest of us to do the same.

"That's what I mean though," Paola said. "There are definitely things that we should do before having sex, like getting tested for any STDs and making sure that our partners are also tested. That's foremost. But once that's done, you're free to explore! Sex is liberating, and a way for adults to play and express themselves" she said, stroking Miguel's beard and licking her lips. "I agree with you," I added. "I also grew up in a pretty conservative family, where sex wasn't discussed without some sort of shame attached to it. Especially sex between people who weren't married. So I grew up thinking that sex was bad or shameful, and it took me a long time to unlearn that. I also heard stories from my married friends who had waited to have sex until their wedding night, telling me that they felt shame for being sexually aroused because of all of the negative things that they were taught about it."

"Wow. I love that you were able to unlearn that way of thinking. And I hope that your friends were able to do the same," Paola said. "I think more people should explore that natural side of themselves, and be loud and proud about it, you know? Do your research and learn what you like and what you don't. But please, for the love of everything that is good, do not go to porn to help you!" Paola emphatically slapped her hand against the dining table.

"Oh man, I wish I knew that," Miguel replied. "So much of what I knew about sex when I was younger was just based off of porn that I had seen. I thought that every man's body had to look the way those guy's bodies were. All ripped and super buff and everything. I compared my body to those dudes and thought that there was no way that a woman would find me attractive because I didn't look like that!" Cardenas' eyes grew wide with shock, as he looked up from his cell phone. "Excuse me, dear" he said, motioning toward Kamryn. "From our interactions this evening, you seem to be quite an intelligent young lady. Do you mind sharing with me your age?"

"I'm 15," Kamryn replied. "Ah, I remember how massive and unknown the world seemed when I was that age." Kamryn smiled her sweet and gracious smile at him. Cardenas turned toward Paola and glared at her over the top of his glasses. "Not only do I find it inappropriate to excuse yourself and make love in the hallways of the host's home while breaking invaluable items along the way, I find it even more disrespectful to speak about pornography in front of this lovely teenager."

The mood at the table grew tense as we watched Paola realize what just happened. As outspoken and bold as she is, she isn't used to having anyone call her out on her behavior. Paola is used to being the center of attention for some reason or another, but this is the first time I've ever seen it be for accountability.

"Mr. Cardenas, I understand that this is the first time we've ever met so there's no possible way that you could have known anything about me before our encounter this evening," she started. "I have no shame about the way that my husband and I choose to express ourselves. I'm aware that it may make some people uncomfortable, but I choose to live my life without shame, unlike most people. Chef is a very dear friend of ours, and if you recall, we apologized for the accident and offered to replace what was broken. My intention with the conversation topic was to inform, educate, and create a dialogue." She took a sip of wine to ease a bit of the tension in the room.

"Despite your intentions, I'm afraid that your behavior and choice of discussion topics has come across as crass and wildly inappropriate. I don't believe I've ever witnessed such behavior at a dinner party, let alone in the home of such an esteemed host. I would hope that your apology to Chef Kababo wasn't limited to the broken statue, and that it also includes your choice to discuss sensitive topics in front of his young daughter."

Paola sat back in her chair with her wine glass in hand and paused for a beat. Miguel rested his head in his hands, while Tory looked back and forth at Cardenas and Paola like he was watching a tennis match.

"What I wanted to convey was that pornography creates false narratives around body types and shapes, and what sex is truly supposed to be. How it sets the viewers up for failure because their brains have been wired to believe that what they see is how it's supposed to be. I wanted to convey that it is exploitative, and extremely low in vibration for the viewer. I know Kamryn is present, and I want her to know that like most things in the media, porn isn't real." Paola said.

"That's so true!" Tory added as he scraped the last bit of crème brûlée from the ramekin without looking up from it. "I thought the girls were all supposed to be screaming and yelling the entire time, and it's definitely not like that in real life". Tory looked up to see all of us looking back at him. "Oh. Were we not talking about that anymore?"

Chef cleared his throat. "Well, with that, would anyone like to join me in the family room for coffee?"

"Yes! Coffee would be great," Miguel said, happy to finally have a subject change.

Crème Brûlée Recipe

Ingredients

Eggs - 12 each (Organic is preferred. You really want those bright yellow yolks)
Heavy Whipping Cream - 946 ml (1 Qt)
Sugar - 200g (1 c)
Fresh Vanilla Bean - 4 pods
Berries - Strawberry, Blackberry, Raspberry, Blueberry

Egg Whites - 12 each
Cream of Tartar - 4 g (1 Teaspoon)
Sugar - 50g (¼ c)
Cooking Oil Spray

Tools

Ramekins 6 - 8 oz
Hotel Pans or Casserole Baking Dish
Mixer & Whip
Mixing Bowl
Butane Torch

Making Crème Brûlée is an easy but delicate process and you will need to watch your temperature while baking because you can totally ruin the experience. Using your mixing bowl you will separate the egg yolks from the egg whites. Traditionally Creme Brulee is topped with whipped cream however in this recipe we will make a simple meringue from the egg whites, totally using all of the product.

To extract the yummy vanilla bean you will need to use your chef knife and split the vanilla bean pod down the middle long ways to achieve this. Once the pod is split, you will scrape your knife against the pod from one end to the other gathering the seeds along the way. Place the Vanilla Bean Seeds into the mixing bowl with your egg yolks. Add your heavy whipping cream & sugar then whisk together until all of the ingredients are mixed well then pour them into your ramekins leaving a ½ inch gap between the top and the custard.

Place the ramekins into the Hotel Pan (or Casserole Baking Dish) and fill it with water surrounding the ramekins slightly past half way. Be sure not to get any water inside of the ramekins.

Have your oven pre-set to 250 degrees F and place the custard inside and allow to cook for 30 - 45 mins. Every oven is different so you will have to watch it closely once the 30 min mark is breached. The custard will become stiff and very little to no browning on the top. Some ovens have hot spots, like the rear is hotter than the front or something odd like that. In this case you will want to rotate the pan midway during the cooking process to ensure even cooking. If you notice the tops are starting to brown they should be finished or your oven is too hot. The ideal is no brown on top but the custard is fully cooked.

Once finished, place them into the fridge and allow to fully cool before preparing the final step.

Meringue

Ingredients

Egg Whites - 12 each
Cream of Tartar - 4 g (1 Teaspoon)
Sugar - 50g (¼ c)

Tools

Mixer
Piping bag (Optional) or Zip Lock Bag (Improvisation)
Sheet Pan or Baking Pan

While your crème brûlée *is cooking you can make your meringue. Make sure your egg whites are room temperature and add them into the mixing bowl along with the cream of tartar. Keep your sugar close by because the timing is super important, if you add it too late the sugar won't dissolve and you will have a bad grainy meringue and if you add it too early it will disrupt the binding of the egg whites. About 1 min into mixing is the ideal time for you to add your sugar.*

I wish I could tell you how long it takes but the time isn't specific when it comes to soft and firm peaks (about 4-5 mins). However, you can tell by stopping your mixer and observing the condition of the peaks on the whisk. If the peaks are firm and holding then you have reached your goal. If they are hanging then you will need to mix a bit longer. Be sure not to over mix the meringue because that is a thing and it will look like cottage cheese with pooling liquid around the bowl.

Once firm peaks are reached then you can place the meringue into your piping bag. If you don't have one of those no worries you can improvise and place it into a zip lock freezer bag and simply cut one of the bottom corner off. Don't feel bad I do this all the time, that's how I know it works! Do be careful when squeezing because the top of the zip lock bag can come undone so don't be a brute okay. Cover the bottom of your baking pan with a thin layer of oil to prevent sticking while baking. Squeeze out mini mountains along the baking pan and place into the oven with the Creme Brulee. The Meringue should take roughly 20-30 mins to set.

The Brulee

Just before serving you will place a thin layer of white sugar on top of your refrigerated custard and in sweeping motions you will apply the flame of the torch caramelizing the top to a golden brown. The sweeping motion prevents burning the sugar which would ruin the dish. Once you have a nice crust you can place your meringue & berries on top to garnish. If you want to get extra fancy you can brulee the meringue as well but that is totally optional! Enjoy!

Chapter 12

The Collective Subconscious

Culinary Arts is very unique in that you complete the entire life cycle every time you perform it. From birth to death. Most artforms don't want you to destroy, but preserve it in some safe place to be enjoyed later. Not with Culinary. In fact, if you don't destroy it the Artist (Chef) is offended. We spend hours and hours planning, preparing, and cooking this food just for the audience to destroy it in a matter of minutes. I think we deserve every right to be a bit loopy at times, because I can't think of another craft that experiences its work destroyed over and over again and finds great joy in it.
– Kababo

The sliding glass doors in the dining room have framed a portion of the endless sky outside, now a deep amethyst as the clouds pass in front of the full moon. Smoke rises from the burning embers left behind from the fire that kept us warm earlier in the evening, now long gone. The toucans have retreated to their homes in nearby hollowed out tree trunks, leaving tonight's soundtrack to the songs of bats and crickets.

As we stood up to leave the dining table, a mahogany grandfather clock standing in the corner of the family room marks the two o'clock hour. No one seemed to notice though, not even Cardenas who had been glued to his cell phone for most of the night. Texting and typing away at his screen, likely responding to angered restaurant goers who disagree with his reviews in the comment sections of the magazine's social media account. He's known for exchanging sharp witted words with loyal foodies after verbally ripping their favorite chef or restaurant to shreds.

Chef and I swear that Cardenas finds some sort of sinister joy in writing those scathing reviews, and that he gets off on the chefs who try to redeem themselves or argue their way into a better one. For being such a decorated and respected chef who once stood at the top of the culinary world, it certainly seems as if he intentionally ensures that the chefs beneath him stay under his thumb. His approval is invaluable to chefs all over the world, and it's for that very reason that we think he doesn't ever give it. After all of this evening's events - boisterous confrontation, actual sex and conversations about it, and an unconventional meal, I wouldn't be surprised if Cardenas gave Chef his own invalidating review by the end of the week.

The rest of us took a seat on the oversized couch as Chef, Dani and Lucas met us in the family room with trays of black matte coffee mugs with golden marble inlays, and a tall black carafe with a mahogany handle. Lucas placed one of the trays on the coffee table in front of the couch, and stood up to see Chef looking at him with raised eyebrows to indicate that he might be forgetting something. "Oh, yeah! Pardon me," Lucas said to the group. "Tonight we have a rare Kenyan Blue Mountain roast coffee. We also have turbinado sugar, half and half, and fresh vanilla sweet cream if you'd like." He smiled at us and offered napkins while Chef and Dani watched him with pride. This was one of Chef's teaching moments and an opportunity to show Lucas that he trusted him, all in one. That's the kind of teacher he is with his students and with the people in his life that look to him for any sort of guidance. He'll explain how something is done, show you, then sit with you while you do it, before he's presented you with an opportunity to show what you've learned. He's surprisingly patient, which is a rarity among chefs, and he's always quick to share what he's learned with anyone in his life who has a desire to learn.

Cardenas was first to reach for the carafe, and poured himself a cup of steaming hot coffee. Settling back into his set, he closed his eyes and savored the sip. "This is delicious coffee, Chef. The only thing that would make it better would be.. " Before he could finish his verbal critique, Dani returned from the kitchen with a tray of pastries. Almond biscotti, butter croissants, vanilla bean scones, and danishes. "Can I offer anyone a pastry?", she asked. The rest of us smirked as Cardenas obliged and took an almond biscotti for himself.

Miguel, Tory, Paola and I served ourselves coffee, while Kamryn called her dad over to where she was sitting, curled up in the corner of the sectional with a burnt orange colored chenille blanket. She motioned for him to tilt his tall frame to her level, then whispered something in his ear. He smiled at her and said "OK, I got you" before heading back toward the kitchen. The two of us made eye contact, and she let a silly smirk grow on her face that let me know exactly what she asked for.

These are my favorite kinds of gatherings. Small, intimate groups of friends - established or newly formed, conversing over late night drinks or coffee. There's something about this type of setting that brings out a vulnerability in people that isn't easily seen in the daylight. We all have a tendency to project an inflated or idealized version of ourselves when we first meet people, but I've noticed that after spending an extended amount of time with others and finding common ground, we begin to feel more relaxed and safe enough to let our personalities show. It's in these situations when I like to suggest a game that helps people to become aware of parts of their lives that may not be evident to them.

"Would anyone be interested in playing a game?" I asked. "Well it's sort of a game. It's more like an opportunity to learn about yourself through a few introspective questions that you won't know the significance of until after you've given your answers."

"This sounds intriguing," Cardenas said. "But, I'm in." Just then, Chef returned to the living room holding a tall sky blue mug, topped with a mountain of whipped cream and chocolate curls that I can only assume he shaved himself. "Umm what the hell is this?" Tory jokingly asked. "I didn't know this was Starbucks and we could make requests!" Kamryn flashed him a sarcastic smile and carefully took the mug from Chef, whispering a "thank you, daddy" in her sweet voice. Chef laughed at Tory's comment, knowing full well that whatever Kamryn asked for that was within his reach, it was already hers. Everyone close to him knows that about their relationship, and it's one of my favorite things to see.

"Alright everyone", I said. "Here are the rules. I'm going to give a prompt, and at several points during that prompt there will be an option for you to make a selection or draw some sort of conclusion. My advice is to go with the first thing that comes to your mind. Know that there truly is no right or wrong answer, and just like life, the goal of the game is for you to get to know yourself better. So the more truthful you are, the better the outcome. Ready to play?" Paola took a bite from her pastry and brushed her hands together to dust away powdered sugar and crumbs from her fingertips. "I'm loving this already!" she said. "Let's do it!"

"This is to write down your answers if you need it," I said as I reached into a small wicker basket next to the sectional and passed around pens and small slips of paper to the group. "I don't need it. I've got it all up here," Tory said,tapping at his temples. Chef laughed at him. "Man, this game can get pretty deep, you're going to want to write it down." "I got this! Trust me," Tory said in a sarcastic tone. Chef raised his hands in surrender with a smile and sat down next to me.

"Okay," I started. "Imagine that you're out for a walk in an idyllic beachside neighborhood."

"A who?!" Tory said with his brows scrunched. Miguel nearly choked on his coffee as he let out an unexpected laugh. "It means rustic and peaceful," Paola said, reaching over to touch Tory's knee in comfort. "Oh, okay. Thanks! Go ahead, B. Keep going," he said with a smirk.

"You're walking through an idyllic and peaceful beachside neighborhood, who are you with? On your way you notice several houses along the path. Are they uniform in size and shape? Or are they very different?"

Paola, Miguel and Kamryn reached for their pens and began scribbling their answers on their papers.

"What time of day is it, and what is the weather like? Is it a bright and cloudless sky, or gray with thunderstorms brewing in the distance? You and your companion continue on your walk, and reach a path that overlooks the ocean. What are the waves doing? Is the water calm and slow moving on the shore, or are the waves wild and crashing?"

"Hmmm," Cardenas ponders out loud. "I have a feeling these responses will indicate something deeper than I expect." I looked at him with a smirk and shrugged innocently. "We'll see," I said.

I paused for a moment to take a sip of my coffee as the group continued to write out their answers. Chef and I glanced over at Tory who had his eyes closed while focusing on the prompt and trying to keep his answers straight.

"You continue to move ahead, and you come across a white horse. How big is it? Is it bridled with a saddle, or walking around freely? What do you notice about the temperament of the horse? Is it wild and bucking, or is it calm and docile?" Kamryn leaned over to Tory and whispered "that means submissive or obedient". "I know that one!" he snaps back to her in jest.

"You prepare to move ahead - does the horse follow you or does it stay put? Continuing along the neighborhood path, you approach a building. What kind of building is it? How large is it? Take a moment to observe the building. What does the entrance look like, and what emotions do you feel as you stand in front of it?"

I watched as the rest of the group wrapped up their responses. "Okay, everyone! Ready to go over your answers?" I asked.

"Yes! I can't wait to see how this goes" Paola said. "Miguel, aren't you finished with your answers, dear?" Miguel continued writing, and paused to chew on the tip of his pen as he pondered what to write down. "Don't think about it too hard," I said. "The best response is the one that comes to mind first." "Okay, okay," he responded. "I'm all set."

"Okay, the person who accompanied you on your walk is either your current partner, or someone that you enjoy spending time with."

"That's what I figured the response would mean," Miguel said. "Who did you write down, my love?" Paola asked . "Chef, of course!". She playfully punched Miguel in the arm, and he laughed, pretending to rub the pretend pain away. "I'm joking! Of course I wrote down your name." "Well my initial thought was my sister, Sara," Paola explained. "But then I thought that the only person that I would want to spend a day at the beach with was my husband."

"Mr. Cardenas, whose name did you write down?" Miguel asked. "I'm not sure that I want to reveal my answers just yet," he replied diplomatically. "That's fine, there's no pressure to share unless you want to," I assured him. "The size and shape of the homes that you saw on your walk represent the way you view life. If the homes were very uniform in size and shape, then you like for things to be predictable and organized. If they were very different, then you tend to enjoy the unpredictability of life, and you appreciate the ebbs and flows that come along with it. You're essentially an easygoing person, and pretty much go with the flow. If you described the weather as bright and cloudless, then you're feeling very optimistic about the current state of your life, and you have an overall positive outlook on your future. If the skies were gray, then there are some parts of your current life that are intimidating and cause you uncertainty or hopelessness."

Cardenas exhaled and sat back in his seat with his coffee in hand, rhythmically tapping the lip of the cup with his finger. "I like this game!" Kamryn said excitedly, likely due to the sugar rush from her decadent hot chocolate. "What did your sky look like, baby?" Chef asked her. "It was bright and cloudless, but it was a little bit breezy because I also saw red and blue kites that people on the beach were flying. What does that mean, B?" I couldn't help but smile at her response. "That means that you're very happy with the current state of your life, and find joy and beauty in everything around you. Not just the major life events, but the little things too." She was beaming at this point, which was a rarity for a typically uninterested teenager. "That's really cool. What's the next one?"

"Now onto the waves. I asked if the water was calm and slow moving or if the waves were crashing onto the shore. The state of the water represents your childhood and how you viewed it. If the water was calm, you had a relatively stable childhood that you enjoyed. You felt safe and secure, and that caused you to want to give love freely to others without expecting anything in return. If you saw waves that were wild and crashing, your childhood may have been unpredictable and a bit chaotic. Causing you to be attracted to unstable and oftentimes unhealthy partnerships and relationships now."

Paola and Miguel looked at each other for a split second before bursting into laughter. Chef and I smirked as we watched them fall over each other as they belly laughed. "I definitely saw crazy crashing waves," Miguel started. "But you know what? I saw the two of us holding hands and watching the waves swell and crash. I'm no expert, but it sounds to me like I find comfort in chaos and can enjoy it with someone who feels the same."

"That's actually pretty common," I said. "A lot of people find comfort in the things that they were used to in their childhood even if they weren't great. The hard part is figuring out if those patterns and environments are healthy or not, and if they serve us."

"So wait, how do we know if they're healthy or not?" Tory asked. "Well, if those patterns cause us to have to shrink ourselves, or make us act out in ways that are detrimental to ourselves, that's usually a good sign that it's unhealthy. If none of that is happening, and you're able to fully show up as your full self in a relationship and even in friendships without betraying yourself or behaving in ways that cause harm or neglect to yourself or others, then great! But if not, it can take some time to unlearn what we were taught, because our brains tell us that's the way that things should be when in reality, the only reason we think that is because it's the only thing we know."

"I never thought about it that way," Paola said. "Growing up, I had a very close relationship with my family, but also felt like I had to hide parts of myself or make myself smaller in some ways so that I wouldn't come off as being too much. It wasn't until I left home when I was about 15 and started traveling the world for work that I learned that not everyone grew up the same way that I did. Tons of family members over to the house all the time, someone always in your business and wanting to tell you what was right for you or criticizing something that you did."

"Yeah that's exactly what happens for a lot of people as they grow older and are exposed to different cultures," I assured her. "For instance, when I was in college I learned that my roommates and I had very different definitions on cleanliness, but that her family spent a lot of time together making memories so cleaning wasn't as high on their priority list. It was interesting. But I'm glad some of these responses are bringing things to the surface so that we can think about them."

I looked around at everyone's faces and was delighted to see most of them in deep thought. "Next is the horse, and this is probably my favorite part of the prompt. When you're walking along the path and you see the white horse, the horse represents the current state of your romantic relationship, or what you'd like it to be. The size of the horse represents - "I know the answer to that one," Paola said, cutting me off. Cardenas let out a heavy sigh. "I'm only joking, Mr. Cardenas." Cardenas adjusted his sweater vest and tugged at his shirt collar a bit.

"The size of the horse represents how you view your partner's presence in your life," I said with a smirk. "If the horse is bridled with a saddle, it means that you see your partner's personality as wild and needing to be tamed. If the horse is roaming freely, you allow your partner to be themselves, and without restriction or boundaries. You enjoy being a safe space for them, and love to marvel at their freedom of expression. The temperament of the horse is how you view your relationship with your partner. If the horse was wild and bucking, then your relationship is likely chaotic and unpredictable at times, and if it's calm and docile, then the relationship is steady and reliable."

"Tory what was your horse doing?, Chef asked his brother." "I'm pretty sure it was calm, but it was also walking around and was kind of curious about whatever was on the ground next to it."

"That's interesting", I said. "That lets me know that you're happy in your current relationship, or you would like to have a relationship where you feel happy but also safe to explore."

"Yeah I could see that. I definitely don't want to be with someone that's controlling or wants to know where I am 24/7. I feel like if I were to be with someone, I'd want us to trust each other but still allow room for us to grow and explore parts of life on our own. Does that make sense?" he asked. "Yeah for sure!" Chef said. "I'm the same way. I have my own interests and parts of my life that are separate from who I am as a dad, a chef, business owner, and a partner, and I think that's important for everyone to have. We aren't here on this earth just to go to work and do the same things day after day. We're supposed to learn and be curious and explore things, and I think it's important to have someone that understands and encourages that rather than tries to control it."

"I wholeheartedly agree," Paola said. Miguel understands that I have a thirst for life that can only be satisfied if I am given the freedom to explore and travel and learn. I love that about him. He doesn't try to control me, but only wants me to be safe in doing so. I've dated men in the past who tried to control me, or they saw my ferocity as something to be tamed rather than celebrated, and they became incredibly insecure. Always wondering about where I was going, or what I was doing, and even if their intentions were good it made me feel smothered and I hated it, "she said as she squirmed and shimmied her shoulders, unable to bear the thought of being under anyone's control.

"The things that we do in relationships with the intention of keeping ourselves safe actually have the opposite effect. So when we try to control and restrict things, it can cause an overwhelming desire to be free. Which is probably why you're so disgusted by your exes, Paola", I said motioning in her direction. "That type of control is basically signaling to you that something is wrong with the way you naturally are, so your response is to rebel and be repulsed."

"So B, what does it mean if the horse followed you?" Tory asked.

"If the horse followed you, that means that you're a natural born leader, and you attract people in your life who trust you and often come to you for advice. If the horse stays put, then you have healthy boundaries with the people in your life, and know when it's time to connect and when to disconnect."

Miguel leaned forward to top off his cup of coffee, and Paola gently laid her hand on his arm. "My darling, don't you think you've had enough? Perhaps you'd like a glass of water?", she said with a sarcastic smile. Chef let out a deep belly laugh and leaned over onto me as he did. Miguel tried to keep a straight face, but couldn't help but join in with the rest of us as we laughed. Even Cardenas chuckled a bit, before quickly composing himself.

"The last part of the game is the building. The size of the building represents your ambition and how assured you feel about meeting your goals. How you feel about approaching the building is how you feel about approaching your goals, and the ease with which you accomplish things in your life. So if you felt intimidated, or maybe even a little afraid, that could indicate that whatever dreams or goals that you have in your life feel out of reach. Or it could mean that your goals scare you a bit, and you don't know

that you even want to accomplish them."

"That's really interesting," Miguel added as he checked over his slip of paper.

"The building that I saw was like a really tall and sturdy fortress looking place, and when

I first saw it in my head I thought wow, that place is really big, I wonder what's inside.

But I wasn't afraid or anything, more so in awe of it and really curious about what was

on the other side of the doors."

"That's really cool! So that lets me know that you have really solid plans for your

future, and they aren't intimidating to you at all but you're more concerned with the

execution and looking forward to it," I explained to him.

Miguel sat back in his seat, clasping the warm coffee mug in his hands as he

daydreamed about the new possibilities that were waiting for him.

"Tory, what was your building like?" Chef asked. "Mine was sort of tall, but it was wide

and took up a lot of space. It almost felt like the size of a school or something because

of how much space it took up" he said. "It was definitely approachable though, and I

walked right up to the front of it like I had a key in my pocket or something. Like the

place was mine."

"Sounds to me like you've got a good handle on what you want to do with your goals, and you know exactly how you want to make them happen. That's good shit, I like that for you. Let's get to work, I want you to get there." Chef said.

Tory tried his best to conceal the joy he felt after hearing big brother's supportive words, but was unsuccessful as his big shy smile spread from ear to ear. Chef was always proud of him, but it was in this moment that he saw Tory as a visionary, much like himself. The way his beloved, sweet mother encouraged them both to be. Before she passed away, she told Chef to watch out for him, and to make sure that he took care of him and guided him. They were very different growing up. Chef, an introverted first born go-getter who never met a challenge that could defeat him. Tory, the baby boy - easily distracted, and flighty at times with a tendency to make excuses for why things were difficult for him. Chef was older by about 17 years, but he made sure to keep Tory within arms reach, even when he was away at culinary school.

"Mr. Cardenas, you're awfully quiet," Paola noted. "How did you enjoy the game?" Cardenas quickly returned his cell phone to his pocket, and adjusted his sweater again. "It was as interesting and thought provoking as I thought it would be," he said dryly. "What were some of your responses?" Miguel asked him. Paola, Chef and I exchanged glances, unsure of what would come next.

"Well, I know that most of you already know each other or have some connection so it would make sense that you'd feel comfortable sharing your responses with each other. However, I feel that the responses are intimate in nature, and I think I might prefer to keep them to myself."

"That's completely understandable," I told him. "No one has to do anything that they do not feel comfortable doing. Like I mentioned before, my hope is that you were able to learn some things about yourself that you may not have realized before playing."

"Yes, well, I'm not sure that the intended outcome was achieved. Nevertheless, I appreciate you all for including me." That was all it took to pique Paola's interest again, and she was ready to meet him head on. "Mr. Cardenas, I can't help but notice that for most of the evening, you've been frantically typing onto your phone, and only engaging in conversation when it's about food or cooking, or when you've had strong opinions about something. Am I right?" she asked as she poured more sweet cream into her coffee cup and stirred it with a tiny spoon. "That would be correct," Cardenas replied. "So that leaves me curious then. We know that you are this world-renowned, well-respected, almighty former chef turned omniscient food critic, but who is Antonio Cardenas the person?" Cardenas let out a sigh and shook his head. "I'm afraid I don't understand what you mean."

"I mean, who are you, really? Who is the man behind the critiques and the sharp tongue? What makes you tick? What do you enjoy about life, and what are your friends and social circle like?"

Cardenas attempted to interject, but Paola kept going in a calm yet sarcastic tone. "But more than that, why are your reviews so harsh?"

"Harsh," he said with a chuckle. "Paola, please" Miguel attempted to stop her. "No, Miguel, I want to know. I think knowing who a critic is in their personal life can only add to the reputability of their reviews, don't you?"

She made a great point, and we all knew it. Cardenas knew it too. Everything he had ever written and published was condemning and analytical, and he has the ghosts of the culinary careers of past chefs to prove it. His reviews were the kiss of death for many careers and restaurants, and he knew it. Restaurants that received even the slightest compliments took pride in the scraps he gave and wore them like a badge of honor, printing and framing the article to hang in their kitchen as motivation.

"Miss, I don't know that I would consider my reviews to be harsh, so much as they are honest! I am a purist when it comes to food and the culinary arts, and if the chefs and restaurants that I review aren't up to snuff, then I believe it is my duty to accurately report my findings to the public!"

"What do you mean you're a purist?" Paola asked in a cynical tone. "I mean exactly what I said. I am a proud student of the most prestigious culinary school in the world, and I have trained under some of the most respected chefs and culinary giants. I know good food. I know how the perfect piece of lamb is supposed to be prepared. I know the exact measurements required to make a perfect croissant, and the precise moment to pull seafood from the fire before it's overcooked. I am a purist."

"And that gives you license to rip people to shreds in your reviews?" "That's exactly what's wrong with this generation," Cardenas huffed. This caught Chef's attention. "What do you mean by that?" he asked. I picked up my cup of coffee to busy my hands as I waited for what would come next.

"This! This is exactly what I'm talking about!" he said, his face beginning to turn scarlet as he prepared to make his point. "Your generation grew up with participation trophies, and being told that you're all special and deserving of every amazing opportunity available to you. Yours is the generation that was told that hard work was unnecessary, and that you should come to expect things to be handed to you just because you are special and unique. It is that very attitude that has contributed to these chefs who wholeheartedly believe that they are the next James Beard just because they can make a decent steak! No! I refuse to contribute to that. I refuse to pamper and coddle these whiny, undeserving amateurs. I've watched too many celebrity chefs - and let me stop right there," he said, cutting himself off.

By this point, the rest of us were in awe of his candor and the passion that was coming from his words. "What does that even mean? In my day, chef was a prestigious and hardworking profession that many people regarded, but it didn't come with flashy television shows or cooking competitions. Now, chefs are like the rock stars of the eighties. They all have crazy tattoos, and bad attitudes and I just don't understand the way the public idolizes them. When you strip away the pomp and circumstance surrounding the so-called celebrity chef, what is left is someone who prepares food for others. That's it. No more no less. The glitz is just a lot of people knowing their names and believing the hype about whatever they prepared."

"My point is this. I understand the hard work, and the grind that goes into becoming a great chef. It is far from easy and a lot of the time, the work is tedious and thankless. But that's the way it was when I was coming up, and it's the way that my mentors were taught, and their mentors before them. I am committed to tradition. Without it, there is no innovation, and I refuse to deviate from it. I don't believe that a trained chef should abandon tradition to make themselves stand out from the multitude of their peers. They should stand out by perfecting their craft, and staying true to those traditions that they were taught so that they can do the same and pass them on."

Chef had been listening intently, but I could tell that his wheels were spinning with a response as soon as Cardenas took a breath.

"I can understand your respect for tradition, and I respect it. I wouldn't have been able to make it through culinary school with honors without that respect. But, I emphatically disagree with your commitment to bashing those who take the traditional ways and make them their own. Tradition is still a guide and roadmap, but it certainly shouldn't be the only way of doing things. Life is about growth, change and movement.

Dead things are stagnant. So in order for the culinary world to keep up with the times, there has to be change. Things cannot stay the same, otherwise there's no art to it. People want to eat food that is exciting and enticing. If they didn't then we would be satisfied with having peanut butter and jelly sandwiches for breakfast lunch and dinner."

Cardenas was visibly puzzled by Chef's opinion, and was unable to hide it. "Well that's a bit of a stretch, isn't it?" he asked Chef. "I don't see how it's a stretch! If there were no creativity in food, then there's no need to experiment with flavor. If the purpose of food is only to provide sustenance, then what's the point of learning different techniques and styles of cooking? I believe that tradition is important, and it's from the foundation of tradition that we are able to build our culinary careers and move tradition forward through innovation. Think about it like this - when I was a kid, I would play outside for hours on end and my parents wouldn't necessarily know where I was. But they trusted that I knew to bring my ass home before the streetlights came on."

"That's the truth." I added. "Our parents were so nonchalant about us being gone for hours in the 90s that there was a whole public service campaign with nightly commercials reminding parents to consider if they knew where their children were!"

"Wait seriously?" Kamryn asked. "That's insane. I gotta see this" she said as she whipped out her cell phone and quickly pulled up a video of the commercial. Tory jumped up from his seat and squeezed next to her to watch.

"You see this? We didn't have the internet when I was younger, and all we cared about was going outside to play and having a good time with the other kids in the neighborhood. Our parents did it, and so did our grandparents before them. That's a tradition. But that's not the case anymore. I can't remember the last time my daughter went outside to play when she wasn't at school. Things have changed, and the old ways of doing things, while still beneficial, aren't the only ways. Kids today are communing via apps and in gaming chat rooms, and while we may not understand it and wish they would get outside more and go play and ride their bikes until the streetlights come on, that's just not what happens a lot of the time."

"I can certainly appreciate your examples of tradition and change, and I agree with you to some degree. However, I am dedicated to the hard work and thorough training that I endured when I was making my mark in the culinary world. Working hard to master the traditions of the craft of culinary, and having my mentors watching over me and meticulously critiquing my work before throwing it out if something was even slightly wrong is what made me such a strong chef and an even stronger critic! I can withstand the pressure and critiques that come with being judged as a chef. Everything that I produced had to be absolutely perfect, and I was expected to prepare the same quality of food every time. Was it difficult? Absolutely! But it made me who I am, and I believe that it is my duty to hold other chefs to the same standard of excellence so that our work and traditions do not fall by the wayside!"

The veins in Cardenas' neck and forehead were pulsating again, indicating his commitment to his statement. Miguel and Paola sat back in their seats, nibbling on pastries while fully invested in watching the exchange as if it were late night television. Chef was still sitting on the arm of the couch next to me, but his posture had changed from relaxed to erect with his shoulders squared in Cardenas' direction.

"That's something that I never understood," Chef started."What's that?" Cardenas asked with a befuddled look on his face. "Why some people brag about their hardships as if it's some badge of honor to proudly wear. As if to say that struggling and surviving difficulties to get to their goals somehow makes them more noble. Who told you that was noble?"

"Well," Cardenas began to speak but stopped short.

"That's ego! Ego tells you that because you yourself struggled or had terrible mentors that only picked your work apart rather than coaching you through mistakes, that your experience was good! And more than that, your ego tells you that your experience is now the benchmark for everyone else that wants to pursue culinary. So you perpetuate that same mindset that undoubtedly made you feel like shit when you were experiencing it, and call it tradition. That's not okay to me! A plant that grows and persists through harsh environments and inclimate weather is no more noble than the plant that was nourished and protected from seed to sprout to flower."

"What is your point, Chef?" Cardenas asked dryly.

"My point, Mr. Cardenas, is that I don't believe that we should project our traumas onto the next generation just because it is our only frame of reference. Just because things were difficult for me when I was growing up doesn't mean that I want that for my daughter. If anything, I want to provide my life for her as a ladder upon which to stand and reach higher heights in whatever area she wants to succeed. Things do not have to stay the same in order to work. That goes for everything in life."

"Mmm.." Miguel said with a raised finger as he reached for another pastry. "I have to agree with you, Chef. Just like our generation has only always known driving cars and using public transportation, but the next generation likely won't have that. I'm sure within the next fifteen to thirty years, all automotive transportation will be automated somehow. Not because cars are irrelevant, but because there's a better way of operating within transportation."

"That's exactly it! Things are always moving forward and evolving, and outdated systems are being replaced with ones that are newer and better. Like, remember when we were in school and had to do research papers? There was no internet to get the most up to date articles and statistics. Everything that you wrote was based on information that was published in an encyclopedia that was printed five to ten years earlier. Information moved at a glacial pace then, and it was the norm to use outdated information and was widely accepted because there was no other way to get up to date reports," Chef added.

"Chef Kababo, I have to admit that you've expanded my views a bit this evening on a few things. While I can appreciate your commitment to progression though, I think we will have to agree to disagree."

"And that's okay with me! I appreciate intelligent and informed conversations, and think that we can all learn to act as a referee in these sorts of conversations. Objectively calling both sides of the game. It's all about perspective," Chef said. Cardenas smiled to himself a bit, and raised his coffee cup toward Chef. "Perspective."

"Speaking of perspective," Chef said as he rose to his feet. "I think now is a perfect time for me to make my announcement." We all perked up a bit in our seats in anticipation. "The reason that I invited you all here tonight wasn't just to share a meal with me, although it has truly been my pleasure to cook for you. Tonight, I am announcing my retirement from the kitchen. This decision isn't something that I've arrived at quickly, and I've spent a lot of time considering how to go about it. But I realize now that the time is perfect for me to bow out. I've been in the kitchen for nearly 15 years, and it's taken a toll on me in a lot of ways, but it's also been extremely rewarding. I love cooking, and everything about the culinary arts, but I don't love that it takes me away from everything else that I want to devote my time and energy to. A lot of you know that I've always had an interest in gardening, and that it's important to me to grow my own food, but there's a lot more to it. I want to experiment with cross pollination and develop new strains of herbs and vegetables. I also want to expand CPC Academy, and teach culinary students and anyone wanting to sharpen their cooking skills. So while I won't be working in the restaurant scene anymore, I'll still be connected to culinary in a lot of other ways but without the daily stress that comes with the kitchen. It'll be on my terms, and I'll have the time and space to be creative in ways that I wasn't able to be before. So with that, I thank you all for your support, and your critiques."

Chapter 13
The Bennu Bird

Michael Jordan's shooting percentage is .497, Lebron James' is .429, and Kobe Bryant's is .447. These guys were the pinnacle of their craft, and yet they missed more than half of their attempted shots. If a chef served 100 plates and more than half were inedible, that person wouldn't be a chef anymore and definitely wouldn't be deemed the best. In fact if we get ONE plate wrong, the consequences are great because our craft can kill you or send you to the hospital for the evening. If there is an allergy amongst thousands of guests, we have to account for that or else the night will be ruined, just like our career. If we burn a single piece of toast, the guest will judge us harshly and I've been in situations where a client called for my resignation for making a simple mistake. Could you imagine the stress and pressure of NEVER making a mistake?

A doctor's profession calls it a practice, and they have protections of that practice when it comes to mistakes. I never heard them calling it practicing Chef while I serve this food that could hospitalize you. The art of taking dead well preserved items and crafting amazing meals is a mastery, and anything less just won't do.

If monetary gain was a measure of skill, chefs should be paid billions or even trillions!
– Kababo

We all sat in silence as we processed the news of Chef's retirement. I knew that he had planned to step away from the kitchen more often so that he could focus on his other ventures and interests, but didn't know that tonight would be his official announcement. I've seen how his time in the kitchen wore him down physically and emotionally, and how hard it was for him to balance his time at the property with everything else he was involved in. He's turned down several opportunities to cook for celebrities and major events that other chefs would have jumped at, but he values his well-being over money and status. To him, there's no point in sacrificing his physical

health and wellness for work and thankfully he's in a position to have that luxury.

"You're really going to retire?" Tory asked. "All I've ever known is you being in the

kitchen or working at restaurants."

"I know man, but it's time to move forward! I've got a lot of things that are in the

works, and I want to be able to devote all the time and energy that I can to make them

happen. Only dead things stay stagnant, remember?"

"Congratulations, Chef K!" Paola exclaimed. "I can't wait to see what the future

holds for you, and I wish you all the success and happiness in the world."

Chef smiled and thanked her. Miguel stood up and reached out to shake Chef's hand. "I

love this for you, man. You're a visionary and you don't let yourself continue to do one

thing just because you do it well. You don't let that define you. I see how you've taken

the root of culinary, and expanded it to be more creative. That's amazing to me, and I

think we can all learn from that."

Chef looked over at Cardenas who had yet to respond to the big announcement.

Judging by the smug look on his face, I couldn't tell if he was pleasantly surprised or

relieved at the news. But either way, his pseudo obsession with Chef's career would

have to die tonight. No more pop-up visits during a crowded dinner rush, followed

months later by terrible printed reviews that would have ruined the career of any other chef. Whatever Cardenas would write about tonight would be the final review of Chef's professional culinary career.

Just then, a glint of morning sunrise peered through the trees in the backyard. The six o'clock hour was marked by the song of the grandfather clock in the living room, and the faint sounds of sprinklers misting the rows of vegetation and herbs in the garden beyond the backyard. The early morning light began to softly pour into the living room, chasing away the shadows from the night. I'm not sure how Chef did it exactly, or even if it was intentional, but everything on the inside of the house looks completely different during the day than it does at night. Maybe it's the positioning of the house, or the shape and design of the structure itself, or the way that the light comes through the surrounding groves of trees in the backyard but it's a curious thing that I enjoy taking in every morning. On the rare occasion that I wake up before Chef does, I like to make a cup of coffee and sit on the couch near the living room window to watch the sun rise and the shadows change.

This morning is a lot different. Chef is wide awake, preparing to see our guests out after a late night. Despite the early hour and their now empty coffee cups, Miguel and Paola haven't lost any energy. They're tucked into the corner of the couch, deep in private conversation, gazing into each other's eyes and sharing laughs as if they only just started dating. Their relationship has always amazed me. Fiery, passionate, unpredictable, but always rooted in love and devotion.

"It's morning already?" Kamryn asked as she sat up in her seat. "It doesn't even feel like that much time has passed, and I'm not even tired." Chef walked over to her and rested his palm on her head, and she leaned into it with her eyes closed.

Paola and Miguel made their way to the front door, saying their goodbyes and giving everyone a kiss on each of their cheeks. Dani and Lucas had finished clearing away the dishes from our late night coffee, and returned from the kitchen to receive their final directives from Chef. He let them know that they had done a great job at the party, and handed them both a small black gift bag filled with his special blend of teas..

"Well, I had better be going," Cardenas said. "I'm going to try to get back to my hotel and catch a few hours of sleep this morning before my flight back to the states later today." He stood up and Chef walked toward the door with him. "I appreciate you coming all this way, and I hope you enjoyed yourself," Chef said with an extended hand. Cardenas shook his hand and nodded his head at him, offering silent thanks. "I can have Brittany drive you to the front of the property if you'd like," he said as he motioned toward me. "Oh sure. That would be great, thank you," Cardenas said. I agreed, and walked out of the dining room door and into the backyard. The air was crisp and cool, and the birds had returned to sing their morning song from way up high in the trees. I climbed into the same golf cart from last night, and drove it from the side driveway to the front of the house. From there, I could see Cardenas and Chef exchanging a few words but couldn't make out what they were saying. Once again, Cardenas' stoic expression didn't give me much to go on either. He walked over to the cart and sat down in the passenger seat, with a demeanor almost as cantankerous as the one he had when I picked him up. I started up the cart and started down the pathway toward the front of the property. The stench of fresh fertilizer wafted through the air as we drove past the garden. "Oh my," Cardenas said, reaching into his pocket for a handkerchief to cover his nose. "Yeah, it's pretty strong," I said. "But you get used to it after a while." I pointed out the garden staff who was laying the fertilizer in the half acre garden. "This is the best time of year to lay the fertilizer," I said. "When the vegetables are at their peak in the growth cycle, and the leaves are finally lush and green after being dormant during the winter. It's an important part of the cycle though, and beautiful to see if you think about it. To experience the full life cycle of a plant, watching it grow from a simple dried seed to a healthy, flourishing vegetable is humbling. Especially considering the circumstances that the plant has to endure to reach the potential that was always inside of it. Inclimate weather, foul smelling fertilizer, droughts, and floods. If after all of that, that tiny dried seed is able to grow, and grow well, then it deserves all of the admiration that we can give it."

Cardenas angled his head at me a bit, then turned to look at the garden as it grew smaller in the distance. We approached the end of the pathway, and his taxi driver was already waiting for him. "It's been a pleasure to meet you, Mr. Cardenas," I said with a smile. He got out of the golf cart then turned toward me and said, "Don't let him get lazy in the kitchen. He's got a gift". He climbed into the backseat of the taxi and I watched it drive away.

One month later -

It was a rainy Saturday afternoon, and Kamryn and I were in the family room stretched out on the couch watching the latest episode of Chef Gods when it happened. He walked into the room swiftly, as if he had been nervously pacing, waiting for test results. He handed me the magazine, folded back to the exact page of Cardenas' latest review without saying a word. He sat down next to me, folded his arms across his chest and nodded his head.

This is what it said:

'Last month, I had the pleasure of spending some time in San Jose, Costa Rica. A major tourism city known for its beaches, tropical climate, and adventurous activities like river rafting and zip lining above the rainforests. The country itself is beautiful; bright and filled with rich culture and national parks that leave its visitors wanting more. Over the last few years though, San Jose has become a hotspot for foodies from all over the world to come and whet their appetite, so it's only natural that ambitious chefs would find their way into the city as well. Much to my surprise, a chef that I have written about a few times in the past made his own move to San Jose, in a bold attempt to open a bed and breakfast on a ten acre property - despite the daunting number of international businesses that fail within the first two to three years. I'm talking about Chef Kababo, who hails from Houston, Texas. After publishing my reviews on his last two restaurants in my column over the span of ten years, it came to my attention that Chef Kababo may have finally taken heed to my advice and found a way to gain access to fresher ingredients by moving to Costa Rica, and thereby finally improving on the quality of his dishes. I was surprised when I received an invitation at my New York office from Mr. Kababo for dinner at his home. The note was short and succinct, providing only the date, time and location for a dinner party. I was apprehensive initially, but sent along my RSVP and made my travel arrangements.

As with all of my reviews, I approach them with an open mind and a cleansed palette. Not expecting to be blown away because that rarely, if ever, happens, but also not expecting to be completely let down. But this night took me by surprise in many ways. So much so that I don't think anything could have prepared me for it. The dinner party included some of Mr. Kababo's family members and staff, and some other very…. colorful… guests that I won't soon forget. The meal was abstract in nature and, if I'm honest, disappointing. A traditional meal should include protein, vegetables, starch, some sort of sauce and a garnish - he knows this, and I'm willing to bet my salary that you, the reader, know that as well. So I don't quite understand how someone with as strong of a background of culinary training could present what he did, and feel resolved enough within himself to call it a "meal". But that's what he did. And once again, like all of the times before, I was let down by his lack of commitment to tradition. The "meal" - and I use that term loosely, was more of a collective of somewhat elevated appetizers. Eggrolls, dumplings, and a crab cake benedict. On paper, the menu reads very flat and unfulfilling. However, I will say that in all of my years of consuming and critiquing food, I have never had an eggroll, dumpling and crab cake benedict like the ones that were served that night.

The eggroll was flaky and crisp with a combination of tart spice and savory, the dumpling was filled with a bundle of joy and the crab cake made me feel like I was just off the boat in Louisiana. It was well cooked and well seasoned, but the flavors and quality of the ingredients were likely due to Mr. Kababo's on-site garden and greenhouse. He proudly grows several varieties of vegetables and herbs, and if I'm not mistaken, I may have overheard him telling one of his guests that he had been experimenting with cross-breeding some herbs to create unique flavors and elevate his food.

Overall, the evening was eccentric and enjoyable, and to the surprise of his guests, came with Kababo announcing his retirement from the kitchen. The announcement came at the tail end of an interesting dinner party game involving pretend scenarios that ultimately sparked vulnerable conversations about the intricacies of our subconscious mind. Kababo credited his retirement to his fifteen year commitment in the kitchen that had a major impact on his physical health, and minimized the time he was able to devote to creative side projects. One of those projects being CPC Academy; a program for up and coming chefs to learn culinary skills from Kababo.

At this point in my other reviews, I hand out my rating based on a four star scale. However, I don't think I can do that this time. Considering that the meal that I was served was eccentric and unclassifiable, I feel that I am unable to rate it based on my usual scale. Instead, I have allowed my experience to lead me to create a new rating, based entirely on creativity, skill, and flavor rather than my usual commitment to traditional culinary values. The rating will be a Gyuto knife, named after the highly sought after and skillfully crafted Japanese chef's knives. These knives are expensive and rare, reserved only for those with the skill to use them correctly. This rating will be used for chefs that are innovative in their approach to food, and are unafraid to step outside of the traditional culinary constructs. With this in mind, I would like to bestow the first Antonio Cardenas Gyuto knife rating to Chef Kababo.
My hope is that he is able to take his skills and invaluable knowledge and make use of them in a way that doesn't disappoint.
-Cardenas

I looked over to see him staring at the ceiling, with his arms still folded across his chest as he was processing the last review he would ever receive from his nemesis. Kamryn gave me a wide eyed look from her blanket cocoon on the other end of the couch. We both waited for her dad to say something. She playfully put her foot on his lap to nonverbally check in with him. I sat up in my seat as he let out a deep breath. "Hmm.." he said, looking around the room. "Sounds about right, coming from him," he said as he took the magazine from my hands. He nodded his head as if to make peace with what he had just heard, then took Kamryn's foot in his hand before dramatically tossing it to the side, making her laugh. He rose to his feet and returned to the kitchen, tossing the magazine into the trash can on his way.

—

Rushcreek
Northborough
Dr
13300
Dr
300